REBOUND REMEDY

CHRISTINE D'ABO

RIPTIDE
PUBLISHING

Riptide Publishing
PO Box 6652
Hillsborough, NJ 08844
www.riptidepublishing.com

Rebound Remedy
Copyright © 2015 by Christine d'Abo

Cover art: L.C. Chase, lcchase.com/design.htm
Editor: Delphine Dryden, delphinedryden.com
Layout: L.C. Chase, lcchase.com/design.htm

ISBN: 978-1-62649-354-4

First edition
November, 2015

Also available in ebook:
ISBN: 978-1-62649-353-7

REBOUND REMEDY

CHRISTINE D'ABO

RIPTIDE PUBLISHING

ABOUT OUR *C*HARITY

Twenty percent of the proceeds of these titles will be donated to the Gay, Lesbian, Bisexual and Transgender (GLBT) National Help Center.

Founded in 1996, the GLBT National Help Center is a non-profit organization that provides vital peer-support, community connections and resource information to people with questions regarding sexual orientation and/or gender identity. Utilizing a diverse group of GLBT volunteers, they operate two national hotlines, the GLBT National Hotline and the GLBT National Youth Talkline, as well as private, volunteer one-to-one online chat, that help both youth and adults with coming-out issues, safer-sex information, school bullying, family concerns, relationship problems and a lot more.

To learn more about this charity or to donate directly, please visit their website: www.glbthotline.org.

TABLE OF

CONTENTS

CHAPTER ONE

The holidays were Cole Todd's favorite time of year. Everything from the smell of homemade cinnamon rolls cooking to the sound of kids singing off-key carols at the mall for passersby. It was the time of year when he could believe in magic and wonder. When he knew good things could happen, and for once he was going to be the one in charge of making sure the holidays charmed the right person.

This year he'd had something amazing planned, something he'd been looking forward to for over a month now: a trip for him and Steven to a ski resort in Banff. Everything had been prearranged. A quiet dinner for two ready to go in their room upon their arrival. Two tickets to the jazz room and a chance to see Diana Krall perform a holiday tribute. Exclusive use of the private outdoor hot tub with the hope that it would lead to sex in the massive king-sized bed.

Yes, he had worked out everything. Scrutinized each detail, ensuring it was perfect. Ensuring nothing could possibly cause them any problems. He'd accounted for everything . . .

Everything except this.

"I know things haven't been great between us for a while, but I can't let you go. I need you. I love you more than anything else in the world."

Those words would have made his heart sing if they were the climax of a movie or a romance novel. They were spoken with passion and longing that would melt the coldest of hearts. Hell, they would have him dancing in the airport right now if they'd been directed at him.

But they weren't.

He was listening to another man—a man he'd never met before—say them to Steven, his boyfriend of six months. Oh he'd recognized Adam Seltzer from the various pictures of him on Steven's computer. Adam had broken Steven's heart when he'd left Toronto for a job in Vancouver. Cole had been there to pick up the pieces. Sure, he'd had doubts that Steven was ready to move on; he'd feared their relationship was the traditional rebound romance and he was the one who'd get hurt in the end. But everything had simply clicked. They'd gotten on so well, so perfectly, that he couldn't help but hope that this time, for once, he'd be on the winning end of things.

Apparently not.

He watched as Adam dropped to his knees in the busy check-in area of the airport, watched as Steven reached out and cupped his former lover's face to stare longingly into his eyes.

"Steven, I quit my job. I've talked to my old boss and they're willing to take me back. Everything is set for me to move back here, to be with you. All I need is a yes from you. I've hurt you. If you've moved on, if you don't love me any longer, then I'll understand. I'll find a way to push you from my thoughts—"

"No baby. I . . ." Steven's voice cracked and tears filled his eyes. "I still love you. I always have. I probably always will." Then he leaned in and kissed Adam.

It was the most passionate kiss Cole had ever witnessed. Steven had certainly never kissed *him* that way. Shit, this wasn't going to end well. Not for him at any rate.

When they finally pulled apart, the small crowd that had gathered around them applauded. Cole didn't know what everyone thought they'd witnessed. It wasn't an engagement or anything—

"I brought this. I'd hoped . . ." Adam reached into his back pocket and pulled out a ring box.

Oh come on!

"Steven Mitchell Cibulskis, would you do me the honor of being my husband?"

Cole wasn't sure, but he might have groaned. Loudly.

Fuck, he'd lost Steven. Though from the sound of things, he apparently never really had him in the first place.

His stomach churned as Steven pulled Adam to his feet and kissed him passionately one more time before embracing him. It was only then that Adam locked gazes with Cole. The other man at least looked embarrassed, though Cole had no doubt it had more to do with Cole being forgotten than the outcome of the scene. Adam whispered something into Steven's ear.

"Oh shit." Steven turned around and looked at Cole. He'd clearly been so caught up in the situation that he'd forgotten about him. "Cole."

There were many ways he could handle this. He could lose his temper, he could cry and whine, he could hand over the tickets and encourage them to go on the trip. It would be a romantic gesture. That's what would have happened in the movies.

He held his ticket a little tighter in his hand. "So, I take it our plans have changed."

"I'm so sorry." Steven left Adam's side and came a few steps closer. "There was no way I could know this would happen."

"I know."

"I didn't plan for him to come back into my life. I thought he was gone for good. That he didn't want me anymore."

"I know."

"If there is anything I can do to—"

Cole held up his hands, his eyes squeezing shut. He'd been hurt far too many times to be overly gracious. "Stop. Please."

"You had plans." Adam's voice made him open his eyes once more. "You were taking him on a trip? Steve, your parents didn't mention—"

"Yes." He swallowed down his anger. "To Banff."

"Can you get your money back?" Steven reached back and took Adam's hand. "Or can we take the tickets and I'll pay—"

"I'll get a refund. Don't worry about it." At least he hoped he could. He wanted to say something else but his throat tightened, blocking the way. With each second ticking past, his emotions threatened to tear him apart from the inside out.

He had to run. Get the hell out of here before everything exploded. "Just . . . Sorry, I need to get out of here."

"Cole, wait!"

He yanked his suitcase behind him, ignoring Adam's, "Let him go. I'm going to take you away. He'll be fine."

Would he? He'd been dumped before and survived. Well, not at an airport on his way to a romantic vacation a few weeks before Christmas. This was actually the third time he'd been left for another man. Did he pick guys who were on the rebound on purpose, or was it simply bad luck? Maybe a bit of both. His family wouldn't tease him, but from the beginning none of them had been big fans of Steven. He hoped his mother and sister would at least wait a week before they started saying, *I told you so.*

The December air was sharp and bit into his skin as he made his way to the Park-and-Go. He wasn't a big fan of the cold, despite living in Toronto, but for once it felt good to be out in it. The wind blew away his anger and numbed his emotions so he could catch his breath. His feet crunched against a thin layer of the snow that had been falling steadily since they'd arrived. He'd been concerned that the snow would delay their flight and they'd spend a long time in the lounge. That they'd lose out on a day of their vacation.

Oh, if only things had been that simple.

The car door creaked as he pulled it open. He should have put his suitcase in the trunk, but that was more effort than he was able to make. Instead he threw it into the passenger's spot, the place where Steven had sat not thirty minutes earlier, excited to head out for their trip and chatting nonstop about wanting to try snowboarding. He was alone, cold, and wanting a drink.

This was like being trapped on the wrong side of a romantic comedy. Holy shit, he was the dude no one remembered at the end of the movie. He was the leftover. The drip no one rooted for at any point in the book. The putz. The loser.

Damn it.

He fell into the seat, slammed the door shut, and turned the car on. The windshield had already frosted, lines of crystals covering the inside glass in long thatched marks. The frost meant another delay while the car heated up. Gripping the steering wheel, he fixed his gaze on the frost, watching as it ran away from the heat that blasted from the vents.

"Fuck!" He slammed his hands against the wheel, the force of the impact elevated by the cold material against his bare hands.

Why did this shit keep happening to him? He should have known things weren't exactly right between them, that what they had wasn't long-term–relationship material. Steven had always willingly followed him and his choices, but never seemed all that committed—like he was simply passing time.

There was something about Cole that kept others away. He was smart, good at his job, generous with his time and money. What more could someone want?

"Maybe I'm broken." His breath rolled from his lips, chasing the words into the dark night.

The cold dampened his anger, bringing it down to little more than a wisp. By the time the window was clear enough for him to drive, he had relaxed. There wasn't anything he could do about the situation. Steven loved Adam, which was obvious to anyone with eyes in their head. Cole couldn't very well get upset, chase after Steven, or even demand compensation for the lost vacation. He might be many things, but he refused to become a villain. Not even at the cost of his happiness.

The highway wasn't overly busy, and it didn't take long for him to make the drive back into the city. Even the traffic in Toronto itself seemed to take pity on him, easing his journey home. He pulled into his parking spot for the condo building, turned the car off, but didn't get out immediately. The thought of going in to his place—totally devoid of holiday decorations because he hadn't been planning on being here for the holidays—made him ill.

What he wanted was a drink.

Maybe more than one.

Leaving his stuff in the car, he got out and made his way down the street to his favorite bar. It was after eleven, which meant McGregor's would be packed. He'd be able to find a spot at the bar, have a beer, and lose himself in the surrounding noises. It would be enough to shake away the pain. At least for a while.

Walking through the doors of McGregor's, he realized fate was working completely against him. He was greeted with a blast of hot air and "White Christmas" playing on the jukebox. Yes, of course, it would *have* to be Steven's favorite holiday song crackling through the speakers. His shoulders slumped forward a tiny bit more as he stepped into the bar and let the door swing closed behind him.

Instead of the normal crowds that filled the place this time of night, the bar was barely half-full. The booths and tables were littered with small groups, folks who were celebrating the season. The only people sitting at the bar were a young couple: a man and woman who were so into one another the bar could have been burning around them and they wouldn't have noticed.

"White Christmas" faded away and was promptly replaced with "All I Want for Christmas Is You."

Goddamn it.

This wasn't going to work. He should turn around and go back to his condo. Nothing good could come from him sitting in a bar and inevitably watching a happy couple make out. He'd half turned when Owen McGregor came out from the back and stepped behind the bar. The bartender looked over and saw him, lifting a hand in greeting. Owen had gotten a haircut since the last time Cole had been there. His black hair was cropped close against the sides of his head, but still long enough on top to tempt a man to run his fingers through.

Maybe someday Cole might get up the nerve to touch it, see if the hairs would tickle his palm as he scratched Owen's scalp.

Oh, that was a helpful line of thought. *Idiot.*

Owen winked at him. "Hey, man. I'll be right with you."

Shit, there went his escape. He waved back and walked over to the opposite end of the bar from the couple. "Thanks."

The only thing more cliché in Cole's mind than wanting to bone a cop who'd pulled you over was the impulse to fuck your bartender against the bar. Owen had starred in several of Cole's masturbation fantasies over the years. Which wasn't surprising given how good the man looked. He didn't have a clue if the bartender was gay or not, but it didn't particularly matter on those nights. Owen was built, had a wicked smile and big hands.

Cole had to adjust himself as he slipped onto the stool. He wasn't wearing the right outfit to hide a massive boner.

Owen had a smile that could make hearts pound, but a kindness about him that made everyone feel special. He was the reason Cole had started coming to McGregor's on a regular basis. Not to flirt with Owen, but simply to be around and enjoy the warmth of his personality. If anyone could help get Cole into a better mood, it was him.

"Surprised to see you here." Owen slid two bottles of beer to a waiting patron, then flipped his hand towel over his shoulder. "I thought you were going out of town for Christmas."

"An unexpected change of plans." The bar seat was hard beneath his ass, offering support as much as discomfort. "Draft, please. Whatever's on tap is good."

Owen grabbed a pint glass and started the pull. "That sucks, dude. Though it's nice to have a friendly face in here tonight."

"I was going to ask. It's pretty damn quiet."

"There's a live band down the street. Some big holiday reunion tour thing. I couldn't even tell you the name of the group, but they're apparently popular. People started leaving here in droves about thirty minutes ago." Owen shrugged. "I don't mind. It's nice to hear myself think for a change."

When Owen placed the glass in front of him, the draft had just the right amount of head on it. "Thanks."

There was something refreshing about swallowing down a cold beer when you were having a bad day. His body instantly relaxed in a way that he didn't want to examine too closely. Steven always had thought he enjoyed his alcohol a bit too much. Which was ironic, since Steven often drank more than he did, with all the careless assurance of a young man who seemed blissfully immune to hangovers. Still, with his tension slowly bleeding away, he was able to calm his mind.

Owen chuckled. "That kind of night, eh?" and topped off Cole's drink. "I'll make sure you don't run dry."

"Thanks." Cole reclaimed the glass, staring at the way the bubbles rose to the surface and popped into the warm air. "My boyfriend, Steven, left me. For his old partner."

Owen wasn't the kind of bartender who normally encouraged a man to pour out his heart. It wasn't that he was unfriendly, quite the opposite, but he was busy running his business. Shit, Cole didn't even know if the other man *knew* he was gay. He looked up to see a slightly bewildered expression on Owen's face. "Sorry. I don't know why I said that. You don't need to know about my crap."

"Hey, it's fine." Owen glanced around the bar, checking on everything before reaching into the fridge below the bar and grabbing a beer, cracking it open, and taking a drink. "It sounds like you need to talk."

Unlike a few moments ago, Owen wasn't quite meeting his gaze any longer. Great. Now that he knew Cole was gay, this was going to be an issue. "Naw, I'm fine. Just wanted a beer before heading home." Swallowing down as much of the draft as he could stomach, Cole left a good inch in the bottom of the glass before slipping off the stool.

"All I Want for Christmas Is You" switched over to "I Saw Mommy Kissing Santa Claus."

"You don't have to go." Owen put his beer down and took Cole's hand. His skin was cool, damp from holding the bottle. He gave Cole a gentle squeeze. "There isn't a problem if that's what you think. I'm more than happy to listen."

Cole's heart ached a bit more at the look of pity coming his way. No, fuck, that was one thing he couldn't handle. "I shouldn't have come. I'm not fit company for anyone tonight."

He was going for his wallet when Owen held up his hand. "On the house. It's the least I can do."

"Thanks." Normally he would argue, or at least toss down a generous tip to compensate, but tonight he tucked his wallet back into his pocket. "See you."

The tension took root in his shoulders once again as he slipped on his coat and trudged toward the door. Still, it didn't quite explain the feeling that he was being watched as he left. When he looked back at the bar before the door closed behind him, Owen had moved off to the side, wiping the bar down as he moved.

Typical. Another example of Cole misreading the situation. Owen hadn't done anything to deserve him being an asshole. Just another reason for him to hide away from people. Pulling up the collar of his coat, he walked through the cold to his empty home.

CHAPTER TWO

One thing Owen truly appreciated about owning a bar was the opportunity to meet all sorts of interesting people. It was one of the perks that helped ease the stress of having taken over running McGregor's after his dad's stroke. Night after night he'd come in, meet with the staff, chat with customers, get local musicians to come play, and generally be able to forget about the rest of the shit in his life. Sure, there were those people who'd had bad days and needed to vent. Hell, he could relate. That didn't mean he would let anyone wallow if he could help it. So he talked to his customers, learned all he could about them so when they needed it he could perfectly distract them.

Bad day at the office? *Dude, the Leafs are actually winning a game!*

Fight with a spouse? *Wow, I need the name of your personal trainer. You look amazing.*

Money issues? *Hey, this one's on the house. Frequent buyer bonus.*

Rarely did he take on the problems of his patrons. He simply didn't have the emotional reserves left for that, and wanted to offer everyone at least one place they could come and forget their troubles.

So when Cole had walked out of the bar two nights earlier, looking as though his heart had been ripped from his chest, it was more than a little surprising that Owen wanted to do something to make the other man happy. It wasn't normally his *thing* to be the soothing type. But he *was* a fixer. Give him a problem and he'd tackle it head-on. Cole was a regular, a nice guy who was normally always looking out for the people around him. Owen had seen him pick up other customers' tabs, slip cab money into pockets, and always generously tip the staff. Not that he was seeking anyone's attention. If anything, he went to great lengths to avoid anyone knowing it was him.

Owen knew.

He'd been a bit surprised when he discovered Cole was gay. Not that it mattered to him. Hell, Owen had slept with guys as often as women. It was more that Cole had always been so buttoned-up, so reserved about all aspects of his life, let alone his sexuality. His out-of-the-blue announcement had thrown Owen for a loop.

And what kind of asshole left someone at Christmas?

The mere idea was a jab to his protective self. If he had anything to say about matters, he'd make sure Cole was in a better place by the time the twenty-fifth rolled around. The only problem was that he didn't know much about Cole, where he lived or worked. The other man didn't come into the bar on any sort of schedule, which would make it hard to nail him down.

Still, he wasn't about to give up.

Saturday night rolled around, and the bar was back to its normal bustle. Owen flew behind the bar, filling orders and shamelessly flirting with anyone who looked him in the eyes. It was a terrible habit to have, but it helped with the tips and set up an atmosphere of fun. People knew that for whatever time they were there, they'd be welcomed and looked after. Not that he had a chance for any action with the patrons. Between making sure that everything was moving smoothly behind the scenes in the day, and keeping the bar tended at night, Owen barely had time to sleep let alone date.

Hell, he hadn't even had sex in . . . shit, eight months.

Ouch, that was painful to even think about.

"Behind you." Jane brushed against him on her way to the bar fridge. "We're getting low on draft."

"I'll drag another keg out in the next lull."

"Oh, that's wishful thinking. And I think we might have a puker in the gents.'" She had the gall to grin as she returned to her side of the bar.

"Where's Moe? It's his turn to clean up." His newest employee had a talent for being anywhere but where Owen wanted him.

"Not sure." Jane twisted off three bottle caps in rapid succession before sliding the bottles across the bar to the man ogling her chest. "I'm sure he'll turn up once everything's back to normal."

Fuck, what was the point of being the owner if you couldn't shove the shit jobs off to the new guys? "I'll get it. Hold the fort."

"Will do." He was so going to read Moe the riot act when he found the little bastard.

Grabbing the bucket and mop from the back room, he made his way down the hallway toward the restrooms. The ladies' had a decent line as usual, but there was no one standing outside the men's. Great, any chance that Jane was wrong went out the window. It explained the recent rush of guys going outside and coming right back in. The alley would smell like piss tomorrow. Owen braced himself for a second before pushing the door open to the one part of his job he hated.

The sound of vomit.

"How are we doing in here?" His normal routine of checking on the drunk was shattered when he looked up to see Cole standing beside a young man who'd had way too much to drink.

"Hi." Cole quickly looked between Owen and the guy. "He's not with me. I came in and found him on the floor. I didn't want to leave him here and figured help would come eventually."

"Yeah, I'd heard we had a puker." Owen stepped farther into the room, shoving the bucket and mop to the side. "But this isn't your job."

"Merry Christmas." Cole gave him a small smile. "I don't mind. I couldn't leave him on the floor."

That tiny twitch of lips did something strange to his stomach. It churned in a way that had nothing to do with the awful smell, and everything to do with the way Cole's eyes lit up.

Damn. He really didn't have time for a crush. Especially with a man who was nursing a broken heart.

"Umm, let's get this kid up before he causes us more problems." He came around to the drunk's other side and draped the guy's arm around his neck. "Mind helping me get him up and out to a cab? I'll give you a free drink for your trouble."

"Sure, though the drink isn't necessary." Cole mirrored his action, resulting in their arms brushing against one another along the kid's back. "Think he has anyone here with him?"

"Probably. Though he might have been orphaned by them. I think he's part of a hockey team who came in earlier, and they all left about thirty minutes ago. Probably assumed he'd wandered home."

They struggled to get the moaning kid up and out of the bathroom. This wasn't exactly how Owen had wanted his next meeting with Cole to go. Nothing cheery, sexy, or fun about dealing with a drunk. Especially one who weighed as much as this one did. The kid started to moan and struggle against them, forcing Owen to tighten his grip. "Settle down."

Ignoring several shouts and taunts from the slightly less drunk patrons, they managed to get the kid outside where Owen could flag a cab. "Want to check his pocket for a wallet? We need to find his address."

Cole patted the kid down. "Yup. Here."

The next thing that happened was something Owen should have expected. As he stepped away to check for a driver's license, leaving Cole to hold the kid upright, the taxi pulled up. Owen gave the guy the address and his corporate number to charge the cab to, while Cole tried to get the kid into the backseat. It was at that exact moment the kid woke up long enough to realize a stranger was manhandling him and decided to defend himself. He roared and took a swing at Cole. The sound of fist meeting face was followed by Cole landing in a heap on the ground, moaning.

Cole shook his head as he sat in a pile of slush and snow.

"Fuck!" Owen lunged for the kid and managed to push him into the taxi before he could take another punch at Cole. "Get this asshole home. And put a twenty-dollar tip on there for yourself."

The driver looked less than impressed. "There'll be a cleanup charge if he pukes back there."

"Fine. You have my corporate number." He couldn't worry about that now.

Cole was still splayed out on the ground looking more than a little shocked by the turn of events. If Owen had been thinking straight, he would have warned him that drunks are rarely happy to be moved.

Holding out his hand to Cole, he gave him a smile. "I think you've earned yourself free drinks for life."

"Wow, that hurt." Cole adjusted his jaw with his hand before reaching up for Owen's. "I'm going to hold you to that."

"Good." If that was all it took to make the other man happy, then Owen was getting off easy. "Let's get you inside and get some ice on that."

Jane and Moe were running the bar when they came back in. Moe cringed when he looked at Cole. He'd been on the receiving end of a drunk punch on his first night, so he knew what Cole was feeling. Owen would have to have a long chat with his young bartender about disappearing during a shift.

"I'm getting some ice," he called to Jane as they walked past. "You two good?"

"All set. I'll make Moe restock." She gave him a shove. "Draft keg. Go."

Cole was surprisingly quiet as they moved through the bar and stepped into the back room. Owen wasn't normally one for silence. His natural gift of the gab served him well in his adopted profession. People didn't come to his bar to be alone. It was a place for music, lively conversation, and cheer. Especially during the holidays.

"I have an ice pack in the freezer. Let me grab it, and you take a seat."

The scrape of the chair being pulled away from the table was the only acknowledgment Cole gave him.

"I'm sorry about the punch. It's a pretty common thing. I used to be a bouncer here when I was working my way through university. You learn to bob and weave pretty quickly."

He turned around to see Cole rubbing his hand along his cheek. A red mark was already rising on his skin, making him look as though he were blushing. It would only be a matter of minutes before the red deepened into purple, marring his handsome face.

Whoa, where had that come from?

Owen cleared his throat. "Anyway. I'm sorry about that. You're wet. You must be freezing."

"It's all good. I'll have to head home and change my jeans." Cole shook his head slightly before wincing. "It's been a while since I've taken a hit like that."

When he handed the ice pack over, Owen made sure to keep from brushing against Cole's hand. "Don't take this wrong, but you don't seem like much of a fighter."

"I'm into kickboxing. Been doing it for years." He pressed the ice pack to his cheek and sighed. "Lot of good it did me tonight. I wasn't expecting him to move like that."

The image of Cole topless and sweaty flashed through Owen's mind. He swallowed hard. "I'm glad your instincts didn't kick in. I try not to pummel the drunks, even if they deserve it. The cops tend to frown upon assault."

Cole held his gaze for a moment, and Owen saw the spark of light flicker, before it was snuffed out. God, what happened to make this man hurt that badly? It had to be more than a bad breakup, though given the time of year that was horrible enough. He didn't know what it was, but he was determined to discover the truth.

"I want to take you to breakfast." The words were out there before he realized he'd spoken. Not that it mattered. It was the perfect idea. "As a way to thank you for your help tonight."

"That's not necessary." Cole was on his feet, the quick movement sending the chair skittering back. "I should probably head home and take some pain pills. I hope this doesn't bruise too badly."

Owen stepped into the other man's personal space, ignoring the way Cole's eyes flashed and his body stiffened. "I insist. I don't make it a habit of letting my patrons get assaulted. And you look like you could use the company. Tomorrow morning. Meet me here at about ten and we'll get something to eat. Or better yet I'll bring something in. I'm a pretty decent cook." When it looked as though Cole would refuse again, Owen lowered his chin and swayed in a bit closer. "Please?"

The smell of Cole's cologne and the warmth of his body seemed to wrap around Owen's cock, stroking it to life. While he'd been with men in the past, it had been many years since he'd had any interest in one sexually. Something about Cole tweaked that side of him, making him want to explore what could happen. It was crazy and completely unexpected. Cole wasn't even the type of man he normally gravitated toward. Or maybe he was. It wasn't like he'd had any opportunity to seriously date, certainly not since he'd walked away from everything to help his dad.

Was he even doing this for the right reason, or was this flare of attraction simply a case of *right place, hot guy*? If ever there was a reason to avoid getting into a relationship with someone, it was that. Cole didn't deserve to be used that way, especially after whatever he'd gone through.

Cole's gaze traveled from Owen's to his lips and back. "I'm not good company these days."

There it was again, that pang of want. He'd never been one to back down, even from his own doubts.

Fuck it.

"Not a requirement." Owen grinned. Shit, it would be so nice to do this. To have someone with him without any expectations or demands. Someone he could talk to, to be a distraction from the pressures of his life. Someone to lean on. "Come on. It'll make me feel better. And I get the impression it'll do you some good to have a change of scenery."

"We'll see." Cole stepped back and Owen instantly missed his warmth. "If I'm not here by ten thirty, then I'm not coming."

"Fair enough." He watched Cole set the ice pack on the table before heading for the door. "I'll see you tomorrow."

That half smile of Cole's came back. "We'll see."

Owen had to adjust his hard-on before going back out to the bar.

CHAPTER THREE

Cole stood in front of McGregor's, his feet having brought him there without his permission. This was a stupid idea. Sure, Owen was an attractive man, and he wasn't put off by Cole's sexuality, but this wasn't what Cole needed in his life right now.

His jaw gave a little throb to remind him of the reason for this particular *bad idea*. He'd been stunned when the drunk had swung and sent him flying to the ground. As much as he wanted to tell Owen that it wasn't his fault—that Cole was more than able to look after himself—the fact of the matter was that Owen was completely to blame for the punch.

When he should have been minding the drunk kid, Cole had been staring at Owen's denim-clad ass.

No man should look that good in jeans. But as Owen had leaned over to say something to the taxi driver, Cole's gaze had instantly shifted down, and he couldn't look away. The next thing he knew, *bam*, his ass was on the ground.

No, being here for breakfast was a terrible idea. He was on the rebound from Steven, and drawn to a man who was simply offering him comfort and support. A good-looking man with a firm ass and a killer smile, but still. Owen probably felt terrible that Cole was suddenly single given the time of year. This was nothing more than a pity date.

Hell, this wasn't even a date!

He should really go.

He reached out and pulled the front door of McGregor's open. "Hello?"

A loud bang preceded Owen's arrival from the back room. "Right on time."

Such a bad idea. "I didn't want you to feel guilty."

"I'm many things, but guilty is rarely one of them." He flung a towel over his shoulder. "I was just setting up the back room for our meal. Figured the staff room was a cleaner spot than the actual bar."

"Thanks for that. And duly noted for my next visit."

"How's your face? I'm surprised you're not sporting more of a bruise."

Cole reached up and touched the sore spot. "I suspect it will be nice and purple by the end of the day."

Owen winced. "I was hoping it wasn't that bad. Come on, I have breakfast ready to go."

Much like he had the night before, Cole gave Owen's ass a once-over when he turned and walked away. At least this time there wasn't a drunk to rudely interrupt his ogling. A pair of ass cheeks really shouldn't fit that perfectly into a pair of jeans. The denim clinging in all the right places and loose around the backs of his thighs—

"I didn't know what you liked so I got us a selection of stuff."

Cole snapped his gaze up half a second before Owen turned around to face him. It was bad form to be staring, especially when he didn't know the first thing about the other man. While he might not have an issue with Cole being gay, that didn't mean Owen wanted his advance either. Better to keep his eyes up and his libido in check.

Not that he had any interest in being with someone else. The end result would be nothing positive for anyone involved. The pain of Steven leaving was still far too raw.

"This okay? I can always order something else from the place down the street if you want."

Cole realized his brain had gone into overthinking mode, which meant his mouth stopped working. The cute, confused expression on Owen's face was doing little to help get his mind back on the matter at hand. Tearing his gaze from Owen's frown—God, it shouldn't be that cute—he looked at the spread on the table.

"Wow." There were scones, coffee, eggs, sausages, bacon, hash browns, and something that looked suspiciously like asparagus. "I think I'll manage to find something I like. I hope this didn't cost too much."

"I had a pile of groceries I needed to use up, and I love to cook. I live, well, really frigging close, so it wasn't a problem making this and getting it here." Owen grinned, pulled out a chair, and dusted it off with the towel. "Your seat, sir."

It wasn't flirtatious as much as he was trying to be funny. Still, Cole's body reacted to the gesture, making it uncomfortable to sit. "Thanks. You didn't have to do all this."

"It's all good. I don't take the time I should to cook properly these days." Owen fell into his seat and grabbed the bacon. "Mostly prepackaged crap when I'm home. Not that I'm home much. I spend most of my time down here at the bar."

"I bet it takes a lot to run this place." A tremor raced through Cole as he reached for the eggs. This was bad. Owen was a nice guy who was simply trying to make up for the unfortunate event last night. Sure, his smiles made his eyes sparkle, and with his shirtsleeves rolled up, Owen's forearm muscles danced. Neither of which was an invitation to get ogled. Cole cleared his throat. "A lot of time and effort."

"My dad did it for years. I'm trying to live up to his reputation. At any rate, it's better than my last job." Owen licked the back of his spoon and winked.

Cole shivered and dropped way too many hash browns onto his plate. "What was that?"

"I worked for an internet security company. Lots of bullshit on a daily basis. Running a bar is heaven in comparison." Owen poured himself some coffee before holding the pot over Cole's mug. "Want some?"

The last thing he needed was caffeine running through his veins. "Yeah. Thanks."

Owen filled his mug, set the pot down, and leaned forward. "Are you okay?"

Cole looked up into his eyes and was blown away by the concern he saw there. This man hardly knew him. As far as Owen knew, Cole was nothing more than a patron who'd stepped in to help him out. The bartender had no reason to take an interest in him or his problems. It wasn't like Owen was hitting on him. He was fairly certain that Owen was straight, or at least straight-acting. Right?

Maybe.

Though . . . breakfast. And wow, those jeans really were tight.

No. The last thing Cole needed to do was unburden himself on an almost complete stranger, no matter how hot or concerned they were.

He opened his mouth to say the expected, *I'm fine, just having a bad week*, but the words that came out instead surprised him.

"I seem to get attached to the wrong men." There was nothing about that statement that would end well. And yet, he kept going. "I'd been dating Steven for six months. He was younger than me, just coming out of a serious relationship and looking for something new. I knew it was a bad idea, rebound romances usually are, but there was just something about him . . ."

He'd been staring directly into Owen's eyes. The flash of pity in his brown eyes hurt Cole, but then it was to be expected. How else would someone feel for a man who'd just admitted to being an idiot? Still, no matter how proper the response was, that didn't mean he had to like it.

"Don't feel bad for me." He ran his hand through his hair before grabbing the coffee mug. "At least Steven didn't cheat on me before he walked away. I've survived worse things."

He had for sure. Steven was only the latest in a string of failed relationships. Not to mention his recent rash of bad days at the office. Owen didn't need any of that dumped on his lap. If anything, this was an opportunity for Cole to forget about all the bullshit in his life and simply enjoy a nice meal with a good-looking man a few weeks before Christmas.

He mustered up a grin and reached for a scone. "Enough of that. Tell me about the bar business. I kept picturing the owner being some old guy who was world-weary."

At the change in topic, Owen sat a bit straighter, his gaze slipping to the food on his plate. "That would be my dad."

Shit. "Sorry, if you'd rather not—"

"No, it's fine." Owen smiled again, but it wasn't as bright. "He had a stroke a few years ago. I took over running the bar so it would stay in the family. I think knowing I was here keeping things going for him helped in his recovery."

"So he's better?" Cole didn't know the first thing about strokes, other than they were no good.

"As well as he can be. He still has his ups and downs, and wants to be involved with the business. The stress of running the bar is too much for him, so I try and limit what he does. It's a fine line between respecting the insights of a man who started this place, and keeping him in the dark so he doesn't get sick again."

They both paused and took a breath. Yeah, this was far more awkward than Cole ever intended it to be. For the first time since he moved into his condo and discovered McGregor's, he really looked at Owen. He had never thought for a moment that the bartender who always greeted everyone with the same level of joviality had problems of his own.

Time to get the conversation back to neutral ground so they could both relax. "So, do you think the Leafs will make it to the play-offs?"

"You're funny." Owen laughed. "Oh wait, you were seriously asking."

Cole stretched his legs out. "Sure. They've had a strong start this season."

Owen crossed his arms and shifted, bringing his foot against the side of Cole's leg. It wasn't a come-on, not exactly. Rather than shift away, Cole kept his gaze locked on Owen's and held still.

Owen picked up his coffee mug and took a long sip. "Yes, but we know how it will end."

"Heartbreak and tears," they both said as one, and laughed.

This was the first time in ages that Cole had felt comfortable at verbal back-and-forth with another person. Steven and he had had to work to find things to talk about. Despite only a minor age gap, they were at very different stages in their lives. Not to mention that Steven hated all things sports, which had never boded well on hockey night. He'd had to DVR more games than he would have liked.

Owen was a forward-thinking businessman, someone Cole had an easier time relating to as he was in sales and marketing himself. They'd bounced lots of business ideas between them in the past. Their conversations, though brief, had always clicked. This morning was no different. They drifted from hockey to politics to the sad state of movies. Before he realized it, two hours had passed and the food was all but gone.

He cleaned the egg goo off of his plate with his last bite of bread. "God, I'm going to explode."

"Happy to help." Owen grinned, leaned forward, and braced his forearms on the edge of the table. "Since your plans for the holidays got ruined, what are you going to do now?"

Owen wasn't quite meeting his gaze any longer. It wasn't an *I don't really want him to tell me* look, more of an *I'm trying not to sound too interested* look. Cole frowned, and for the first time since they'd sat down he wasn't sure where exactly the conversation was going.

"I'm sure my parents will take pity on me." He'd already called his mom to give her the bad news. She'd extended the invitation for him to join them before he'd even finished telling her about the breakup. It wasn't exactly the sort of consolation prize he was interested in, but it was better than being alone. "Nothing like dry turkey and too much wine to pass the time. Though that will just be Christmas day. I have time off this week so I'll probably sleep in and do some Christmas shopping."

Owen cocked his head to the side, and gave a little nod. "I see." Then he cleared his throat and sat up a bit straighter. For a moment Cole thought he was going to stand, but instead he looked him straight in the eyes. "What if I had an alternative to offer? Something a little extra for you on your days off?"

Cole flexed his hands, fighting the urge to push away from the table. He knew what Owen was about to offer, even without hearing the proposal. "I think that would be a bad idea."

"You didn't even hear my suggestion." Damn it, he sounded disappointed. And he was pouting.

"I'm sure it involves hanging out with you. Maybe going to supper or a show. Or even to your place for a drink. Then there'd probably be sex or something to help me forget my troubles."

Owen chuckled. "You say that like it's a bad thing."

"Are you gay or bi?" He cocked an eyebrow, knowing exactly the look he was projecting. "I haven't figured that out yet."

"Bi."

"When was the last time you were with a guy?"

"University." Owen frowned. "I think. There was one night a few years ago when something might have happened. Not sure because tequila. Lots of tequila."

"Look, I've just gone through one rebound relationship, the last thing I need is to get into a pity-fuck situation. You're an attractive guy, but you don't need my shit dumped on you." He pushed away from the table, as something that felt strangely like regret curled in his chest. "Thanks for this, though. I'm glad I took you up on it. It's a nice reminder that there are still decent people out there."

On impulse, he stuck out his hand for Owen to shake when he stood and moved to join him. A few uncomfortable moments passed before Owen got to his feet and accepted the handshake. "Anytime."

What happened next was something Cole was far from expecting. One moment they were shaking hands, the next Owen pulled him close. Their mouths were only inches away, making it difficult for him to breathe. He was surrounded by the scent of the other man, the heat from his body. Even without touching, he could feel Owen's strength, the muscles that lurked beneath the tight shirt and well-fitted jeans.

He sucked in a tiny breath, which only gave him another burst of Owen. "What are you doing?" His words were little more than a whisper.

"Shaking your hand." Owen tightened his hold slightly. "What does it look like?"

Cole should have pulled away, protested, something to put the other man in his place. He didn't.

Owen leaned in closer, but somehow kept his lips from brushing Cole's. They were close enough in height that it would have been easy to kiss. A slight tilt of the head and *bam*, contact. But that wasn't happening. He shallowed his breathing, not wanting to become overwhelmed by the sheer potency of the bartender. It wasn't exactly working.

In fact, he was failing miserably.

"I hate to see you unhappy." Owen spoke the words softly, but they penetrated hard. "I've watched you many nights at the bar. You smile, but you've never seemed . . . right. Happy."

He had no words to respond.

"I won't stand by while someone is miserable, especially this time of year."

"I'm not your responsibility."

"I know. Doesn't mean I'm going to give up on you."

For a heartbeat, Cole thought Owen would give in to the blinding heat that had flared between them and kiss him. He even held his breath as his lids started to slide shut. But as quickly as the moment came, it was shattered when Owen took a step back and released his hand.

"Asshole," Cole whispered, his body shaking from the encounter.

"Maybe. But I get the impression my advances aren't exactly wanted."

He couldn't be certain, but it sounded as though there was an unspoken *yet* at the end of that sentence. He hated that the other man could already read him. "I better go."

"Sure." Owen didn't move, didn't look away.

"Thanks for breakfast." He wanted to leave, but his feet wouldn't cooperate. He was rooted in place.

"Anytime." Owen's lips curled into a smug little smirk. The sparkle in his eyes that had disappeared earlier was back.

Lust warmed Cole's chest and spread downward until his cock was hard in his pants. This was stupid. He shouldn't be attracted to a man he barely knew, a man who had issues of his own and was more than likely a workaholic. Spending time with him would lead to awkward encounters and things that they'd both end up regretting.

"I thought you were leaving?" Owen cocked his eyebrow as he murmured the words.

Cole swallowed. "I am." *As soon as I remember how to walk.* "I'm not looking for another relationship."

"I'm not either. I don't have time for one." Owen tilted his head. "But hey, maybe you could use the company. And quite frankly, I could use a bit of time to myself. You'd be doing me a favor."

"By doing what?" *Such a bad idea . . .*

"Well, it's fourteen days before Christmas Eve—"

"Seventeen."

"Close enough. On the weekend we'll go out and have some fun. Maybe we can do a bunch of things, a few every day or two. Something to make up for the shitty breakup for you, and a chance for me to get away from the bar for a bit."

"Sex?"

"You have that on the brain or something?" Owen laughed. "No, just two guys hanging out. I'll come up with some stuff. You come up with some stuff. It'll be fun. No pressure to perform, to do anything that you're uncomfortable with."

It had been a long time since Cole had bothered doing something just for the hell of it. Steven used to tell him to lighten up, that he was always too serious. It had been one of the reasons he'd wanted to take him to Banff, to prove that he could be as fun as anyone. Well, Steven wasn't here now, but that didn't mean that he couldn't go for it.

"Fine. I'm game." Without thinking about it, his body swayed closer to Owen's. *Shit, too close.* He stepped back and cleared his throat. "I'll leave you my number." Grabbing a pen and a napkin, he quickly scrawled his cell number down. Owen still hadn't said anything about the near kiss, and that was probably for the best.

When he stood up and held out the napkin for Owen, the other man was looking at him with a strange expression. "Thanks. I'll text you tomorrow with the details."

"Sounds good." This was worse than the first time he'd gone out with a guy on a date. "Thanks again for breakfast."

"Thanks again for helping me with drunk duty. I hope your face is feeling better soon."

"Better already."

"I'll see you out."

Owen walked him to the front door. The short journey across the bar was the longest minute in his memory. Maybe he was hard up for sex if he'd become this aware of another man's body, smell, heat, in such a short span of time. Without stopping, he moved past Owen and opened the door.

"Cole?"

He stopped, one foot on the sidewalk, and turned to look over his shoulder at Owen. "Yeah?"

"Next time you have the urge to kiss me"—Owen threw him a wink—"you don't have to stop."

With his face flushed, Cole bolted for his condo.

CHAPTER FOUR

Owen delegated the opening of the bar to Moe and spent some time in his office trying to come up with ideas for his spontaneous invitation for Cole. What the hell had he been thinking, offering to plan multiple days of distractions for them? He didn't know what to do the first afternoon, much less plan out a bunch of events.

He'd been thinking with his dick, that much was certain.

Thank God he had a week to come up with something. If he had a better sense of who Cole was as a person, then perhaps this wouldn't be such a monumental task. Shit, he didn't even know if Cole had simply been humoring him, or had been so wrapped up in the moment that he agreed without thinking. He was certain that he'd get a polite *Sorry but I've changed my mind* once he eventually got around to texting him.

If he ever managed to come up with an idea better than bowling.

Who the hell bowled anymore?

With any luck, Cole did.

A knock at his office door drew his attention. "Hey, boss." Moe gave him a small smile, but didn't brave coming into the room. He was still in the doghouse after having disappeared the other night, and Moe knew it. "Just wanted to see if you were coming out, or if you're going to be in here for a while?"

"What time is . . . Shit!" Owen jumped to his feet, sending his chair scraping across the floor. "I'm coming."

"It's all good. Jane checked on you a few times and said you looked pretty focused. We've got it handled if you're working on something." Moe shrugged. "We just wanted to make sure everything was okay."

"It's good." He ran his hand through his hair and huffed. "Just trying to come up with an idea on how to help a friend." Was Cole a friend? It was easier than trying to say *hot guy who might be attracted to me and whose cock I wouldn't mind sucking.* Much more straightforward.

Moe took a tentative step into the office. "What's your idea so far?"

He didn't need to look down at the list to know what was written there. "Bowling."

"What's wrong with your friend?"

"Bad breakup."

"Bowling is good." Moe shrugged. "So is getting shitfaced while watching a holiday horror movie."

Owen grabbed his pen and jotted that down. "I don't even know if he likes horror. But it's worth a shot."

"Is this for that guy who was here the other night? The one who got punched?"

"Cole. And yes."

"Oh."

Owen looked up and narrowed his gaze. "What?"

"He's gay, right?"

"Yes." God, he hoped this wasn't going to turn into a thing. He actually liked Moe and really didn't want to have to fire him for something stupid. "Problem?"

Moe's eyes widened, and he held up his hands. "No way. I don't know the dude. And you . . . don't date. Never seen . . . I just thought that would . . . trying to come up with some ideas. That's all."

Owen knew Moe was a good kid, he just had a nasty tendency to stick his foot in it more than most. And he was right that Owen hadn't dated anyone in the six months that he'd worked here. Shit, it really had been a long time for him. "Thanks. I think you should go check on Jane. I don't want her being out there alone."

"Yup. Will do." Owen hadn't seen Moe move that quickly since the day he'd hired him. It would have been funny if he weren't in a mood.

What the hell had he gotten himself into?

Something he hadn't done in a long time, apparently. Hauling out another piece of paper, he quickly scribbled down *lube* and *condoms*.

He was still struggling with his nonexistent list when the phone rang. Without looking at the caller display, he picked it up. "McGregor's."

"You're in the office? Why aren't you out at the bar? The evening crowd should be there by now."

Owen closed his eyes and managed to suppress his sigh. "Hi, Dad. How are you doing?"

"Well? It's past eight and that's when the crowds start to pick up. Things haven't changed that much."

"I know. Jane and Moe are working the bar, and everything is fine."

"You can't trust those kids with the business. God only knows what they'll get up to. You need to be out there watching them to make sure they don't do anything stupid."

"I know because I hired them. Everything is fine. Promise."

This was how their conversations mostly went these days. His dad would criticize, and Owen would get defensive. He hated that their relationship had come to this, especially considering how close they'd always been. He wanted to blame the change in his dad's behavior on the stroke, but he knew there was more to it than that. His father's depression had kicked up several notches since he'd officially retired from running McGregor's. Owen couldn't imagine how hard it must be, having no other option than to walk away from a life's work.

Patience and love. That's what his dad needed, and he'd be dammed if he'd give him anything but that.

"So what has you calling tonight? You looking to come down and check on the old place?" He hoped not, but sometimes that helped his dad get out of his funks. "You know I always have your Guinness on tap."

"You damn well better. A bar's not a bar without Guinness." There was an odd note to his voice. He cleared his throat. "Not coming down tonight. Just wanted to check in. It's month's end."

Ah. "Yes, I've been on the accountant to get the report done up. She's supposed to send you a copy. You know I like you to give everything a look over to make sure those numbers line up."

"Well, she hasn't. I don't like her. She treats me like an idiot."

Cammie was Owen's friend from Black Shield, the security company he'd worked at before McGregor's. Warm and fuzzy weren't words normally associated with her, but she was the best accountant he knew. "Dad, she treats everyone like an idiot. I'm fairly certain she's a genius or something."

The huff came through loud and clear. "It's still my name on the bar. I want to make sure you're not running it into the ground."

It's my name on the bar too. Owen dropped his forehead to the edge of the desk. "Give me some credit. You raised me in this bar. I wouldn't let anything happen."

Another grumble.

"Dad, if I have a problem with anything you know you're the first person I'm going to ask."

"Bullshit. You and your mother are trying to keep me as far away from there as possible. You wouldn't mention a problem ever."

"Dad—"

"There's something wrong right now and you haven't said a fucking word."

Owen heard his mother's admonishing, "Jason, language!" in the background. He chuckled. "You're in the shit house now."

"Well, it's true." He'd pulled the receiver far enough away that Owen knew the comment was directed toward them both. "Don't try and deny it; I can tell from the sound of your voice. It was just like how you sounded working for that shit-hole company. Now what the hell's the matter?"

"It's a personal thing, nothing to do with the bar. Promise."

"Man or woman?"

His dad was an old-school kind of guy. They'd had a long conversation Owen's first year of college when he realized he was attracted to men as much as he was to women. Despite his dad not *getting it*, he'd been surprisingly open-minded about the idea that his son might bring a man home. That said, it wasn't something they talked about, even if Owen knew he had his parents' support.

"Dad . . ."

"Must be a man. You never hesitate when it's a woman."

The next thing he knew his father's voice was replaced by his mother's.

"Owen, baby?"

"Mom." God, this so needed to end. "I need to get out to the bar."

"Don't go lying to me. You just told your father everything was under control. Now, who's this man and what's the problem?"

There were two ways this conversation could go: Owen could deny there was a man until his mother wore him down with kindness and guilt, or he could spill the details now and save twenty minutes.

Option B it was. "I met a man. Just a friend, but his boyfriend left him a few days ago for his ex."

"What a horrible thing. And you want to make him feel better. That's so sweet."

"Not sweet." He'd rarely been accused of sweetness. "Just looking after a good patron."

"Buy him a beer!" his dad shouted in the background.

"Hush, Jason. Now, what were you thinking?"

He gave her a quick rundown of what had happened. "I have bowling on the list. And watching a horror movie."

"Ugh, terrible things. Try skating."

"He might not skate."

"Easy to learn. Oh, and there's a series of wonderful holiday tours at some of the local breweries. He might enjoy going to one of those. I think I saw your friend Xander's place listed."

Within five minutes, he had a list with more ideas than he'd have ever been able to come up with on his own. "That's awesome, Mom."

"My pleasure, dear. If you want to bring your friend over for drinks, you're always welcome. It would be nice to see you out with someone for a change."

"It's not like that." He didn't know Cole well, but being brought home to meet the parents would undoubtedly freak him out.

"Of course not." He hated when she used that tone. "Let me know how you make out."

"I will. Love you and Dad."

"Love you too."

He hung up the phone and stared at his list. Shit, there were some really good ideas here. Things that friends would do together, buddies hanging out having a good time. Sure, there were a few that might be considered romantic if framed in that light, but he had no intention of doing that.

No way. This was about trying to cheer up a friend over the holidays.

It had nothing to do with wanting to see Cole smile.

Or wanting to lean in and kiss him, just to satisfy his curiosity about what the man would taste like.

"Fuck." Owen shoved the list into his desk, slamming the door shut.

This was stupid. Cole didn't really know him. Yes, there'd been some mutual attraction between them, but then again Cole had just had his heart stomped into a thousand pieces. He didn't want a rebound romance any more than Owen wanted to be the reboundee.

Dumb.

He picked up his cell phone and stared at the blank screen.

Stupid idea.

He thumbed through his contacts until he came to Cole's name.

Thinking with your dick again.

He hit the text message icon and sent the information about the beer tour—tomorrow afternoon at three—before tossing it back onto his desk. There, he'd done what he'd promised and the ball was now in Cole's court. Chances were he'd get a polite rejection and that would be the end of—

His phone buzzed, and he picked it up before his brain registered what he was doing. It was Cole, and his response made Owen grin.

Tomorrow sounds good. I've always wanted to go on one of those tours. I'll meet you there.

He had a date. No, not a date. He couldn't think of his outings with Cole as dates. That way only led to heartache and binge-eating pizza.

He had an adventure. One of many with his new friend. Friend? More like buddy. Yes, that was better. Two buddies hanging out and having a good time, and nothing more.

Yup.

He drummed his fingers, momentarily mesmerized by the rhythmic thudding. When Cole's face flashed through his head—a small smile and a sparkle in his eyes—Owen pushed himself to his feet and marched out to the bar. He couldn't afford to distract himself with thoughts of the other man. Not when he had a bar to run. Tomorrow . . . he'd work out the details for their get-together then.

Just friends.

That's all this was.

CHAPTER FIVE

$\mathscr{C}$ole didn't quite know how to dress for a brewery tour. He'd stood staring at his closet for a good ten minutes before he finally slipped on his jeans and a long-sleeved crew top. This wasn't a date, so there was no reason for him to put a lot of effort into his appearance.

So what if he spent a few extra minutes on his hair and took care to shave nice and close? It wasn't as though he and Owen would be making out or anything; he simply had the extra time to put some effort in. There was nothing wrong with taking pride in his appearance.

That's all it was.

The storefront of the Steel Anvil Brewery was bursting with holiday decorations. He stepped through the door and was greeted with the sight of a large anvil wearing a Santa hat and wrapped in garland. The smiling Grinch doll must have been an afterthought, set haphazardly on the anvil's edge. A group of guys who looked to be in their early twenties were taking pictures in front of the anvil. They stopped and stared at him as he came in.

He nodded and quickly moved past in search of Owen.

The room was already full of people, small groups milling around looking at the brewery's merchandise and laughing. They were all smiling and carrying on as though they didn't have a care in the world. The lump that had taken up residence in his stomach rolled, making him as annoyed as he was nauseous. There was no reason for him to be nervous for his not-really-a-date.

"Cole!"

At the sound of Owen's voice, he stood a bit straighter. It took him a second to find the other man, but saw him as a group of twenty-something girls moved away from the bar.

Today might have been nothing more than two friends getting together for some fun, but his cock still took interest at the first sight of him. Owen was also wearing jeans, the same ones that Cole had been ogling his ass in the night he'd gotten punched. But rather than the tight T-shirt he normally had on behind the bar, today Owen had put on a navy-blue button-down. He'd left the collar open, giving Cole a glorious view of his neck.

Shit.

Ignoring his libido, Cole slipped off his jacket and hung it up on the coatrack before making his way to Owen. "Hey."

Owen was leaning against a long counter that held a cash register at the end. He'd been talking to a bear of a man with a large hipster beard and forearms covered in tattoos. Hipster man was hot. His eyes were a crystal blue that felt as though it could pierce Cole's soul when directed at him. He was the type of man Cole normally fell for instantly. It was weird, but he didn't feel the same sense of ease looking at him as he did with Owen.

"Cole, this is Xander. He's one of the brewmasters here at the Anvil. Xander, this is my knight in shining armor, Cole."

Xander held out his hand, and Cole did his best not to hold his grasp for too long. Xander's hands were big and strong, though not as long as Owen's. "Nice to meet you. I see you're still sporting a bit of a shiner there."

Cole touched the sore spot on his cheek. The bruise thankfully hadn't darkened much more and would no doubt fade quickly. "Yeah. Who knew a drunk could hit that hard."

"Owen here does. Bastard should have warned you." Xander chuckled. "I'm just teasing. Every tour participant gets a free half-pint just for showing up. What can I get for you?"

The most Cole knew about beer was that he preferred it cold. Looking to Owen, he cocked an eyebrow. "You're the expert. What do you suggest?"

Cole shouldn't have enjoyed seeing the sparkle in Owen's eyes.

He did.

"You don't seem to like the dark stuff. They have an IPA here that's outstanding. That's what I'm drinking." To punctuate his point, Owen lifted his glass to his lips and swallowed.

Cole watched the ripple of his throat as the beer went down. Owen's neck was thick and muscular. Not ripped like someone who spent too much time at the gym, but with just enough muscles that Cole had to fight the urge to lean in and steal a taste. "Uh. Yeah. Sure." *Brilliant conversationalist you are.*

Xander's gaze drifted between them before his smile widened. "Coming up. You can drink it while you're on the tour, so no need to rush."

"Thanks." Cole looked around after accepting his glass. "This place is cool."

Owen nodded toward one of the display units. "Let me show you around."

Cole couldn't shake his nerves as Owen walked beside him. God, a week ago he'd been happily involved with Steven and looking forward to spending time at a resort. The thought that another man—especially one he barely knew—could so completely capture his attention was a bit terrifying.

It had to be the rebound effect. Nothing more. Because, really, who fell in love with someone else that quickly?

He cleared his throat and looked back at where Xander was now chatting with an older couple. "So I take it the two of you are friends?"

Owen grinned but didn't meet his gaze. "You could say that. We dated about eight years ago."

"Oh." Cole drank the rest of his beer in one gulp. "I didn't know."

"How would you?" Owen leaned over a display case that held a series of tubes and glass thermometers. "This isn't some weird meet-my-ex thing. Xander and I have been nothing more than friends for ages. When somebody told me his microbrewery was on the list participating in the holiday-tour-bonanza thing, I figured this was the best place."

It shouldn't have crossed his mind, but the moment Owen said *ex*, the word conjured Steven's face. "It's good that the two of you are still friends. Not everyone can say that."

"Shit, I'm sorry." Owen placed a hand on his shoulder and gave a gentle squeeze. "I'm an ass. I didn't think."

"No, this is good. It's good to have the reminder that a breakup isn't the end of the world." Even if it felt that way. "I'm sure I'll have to see Steven again at some point. I'd like to think that I'd be able to be his friend."

Probably not.

Owen's hand lingered on his shoulder, and Cole wasn't about to encourage him to move. It was a completely different sensation being touched by him than it had been when Steven was close. For whatever reason, Cole had felt the need to be the dominant one when he was with Steven. Steven would look to him to make the plans, arrange the transportation, book the restaurant reservations. He'd assumed at the time that Steven enjoyed having someone look after him, but now he realized there'd been more to it than that.

Steven still had been in the throes of his breakup throughout the duration of their time together. When the pain of heartache weighed down on you, it was difficult to make decisions. He had done for Steven what Owen was now doing for him: taking the lead and making sure there was nothing to worry about.

The difference was, he knew what Owen was doing for him was temporary. With Steven, he'd never been given the option to be anything other than provider. Not once did Steven take Cole's needs into account. It was weird he hadn't realized that before.

"Hey, you okay?" Owen let his hand fall away, and Cole immediately missed the contact.

"I'm good." He wasn't going to let anything ruin today. He reached out and cupped Owen's elbow. "I needed this. Thank you."

The spark that ignited in Owen's eyes held more than simple pride. There was a heat behind it that caused Cole's skin to prickle with awareness.

"If I can have everyone's attention." Xander clapped his hands loudly. "We're going to start the tour. Please follow me into the tank room. Please keep together and be careful not to touch anything. There isn't a lot of room once we all crowd in. It's also quite loud with the cooling equipment, so I'd ask if you could keep the chatting down until we get to the bottling room. Thanks so much and here we go."

Cole moved forward with Owen just behind him. It was strange how quickly he was becoming aware of Owen's presence; the scent of him, the feel of his body heat against him, the inexplicable craving for physical contact. It shouldn't be this difficult to keep from leaning back so that they were pressed together.

This wasn't a date.

He didn't want a boyfriend.

Shit, he was still dealing with a broken heart.

The crowd was herded into a large, cold room that housed gigantic metal silos. A shiver passed through him and goose bumps rose on his skin despite being covered. Xander stepped up on something so that he was visible to the entire crowd. Good, he needed a distraction, something that would take his mind off of Steven, Owen, and the budding hard-on that was threatening to make his pants far too tight.

"Welcome, everyone, to the heart and soul of the Steel Anvil Brewery. This is where we make our beer." Xander's voice cut through the hiss and hum of the machines. "Think of what you're seeing here as a giant six-pack. Each one of these silos contains a different batch of one of our brews."

A small woman behind them pushed forward and tried to move through the crowd. The rejigging of the group forced Owen closer so that he was now pressed chest to shoulder, groin to ass against Cole.

"Sorry." Owen's breath heated his ear and the side of his neck. "Not a lot of room here."

Fuck.

His cock was now fully hard. The sea of bodies in front of him and the press of Owen's hip against his ass from behind gave him nowhere to retreat. He cleared his throat and tried to focus on Xander's presentation. Yup, the man's mouth was moving, which should indicate that words were coming out, but Cole's hearing had abandoned him.

"You're tense." Owen had moved his mouth close to his ear so only Cole would hear his whisper.

"I'm listening." Well, pretending to listen.

Owen placed a hand on Cole's hip. "That's good. Xander's an interesting speaker."

Xander clapped again. "Okay, if you look up, you'll see the large glass window. That's actually a retractable window. It's how we bring the barley into the building so we can load it directly into the hopper."

With his head tilted up, the side of Cole's face came in line with Owen's mouth. The scent of cologne hit him hard, as did the light brushing of their faces.

He swallowed hard. "You're not looking."

"I'm looking." Owen tightened his grip on Cole's hip. "I like what I see."

Jesus.

"Everyone keep together. We're now going to go up these stairs and I'll show you the kettle."

The last thing he wanted was to get any hotter than he was already. He moved quickly forward, bumping into the woman who'd forced him and Owen together earlier. "Sorry."

She ignored him.

The tour continued on that way. The crowd would shuffle along, Xander would stop and talk, Owen would come up behind Cole and lightly touch him. The cool air did nothing to douse his arousal, nor did the heated looks Owen sent his way. When they finally went into the basement where the capping machine was housed, Cole was ready to push Owen against the wall and rub off against him right then and there.

Xander stood on a small box and crossed his arms. "This machine is our lifesaver. It washes, fills, labels, and caps every bottle of beer that comes out of Steel Anvil. Believe it or not, we used to do this by hand. The tall, handsome man standing in the back there used to help. He would partake of too many samples, so I had no choice but to buy this beauty and fire his ass. I had to save some money."

The crowd laughed and most turned to Owen.

"Hey, I wasn't being paid. I had to get something for my efforts. It was a fair wage."

Cole slid his gaze away as Owen beamed at the group. He was even more handsome when he smiled that way. It was the same look he'd give people when he was behind the bar. Cole used to think he was flirting, but that wasn't it at all. Owen had a warmth that brought something extra to everything he did.

"We'll head back upstairs to the showroom where you can purchase any of our beers from the cooler. We also have a few l imited-edition brews that you might be interested in for the holidays. You won't see them again until next year."

The group moved back to the stairs while Xander came over to where they stood. "I'm glad you two were able to come."

Owen put his hands on his hips and grinned. "Are you kidding? I love checking out what you're doing next. I'm always amazed at how far this place has come. Xander started this up with his cousin right out of college."

"I realized that my hobby of drinking beer was a good education for making my own. Somehow the bank agreed and gave me a loan."

It was strange being on the outside of what was a long-lasting friendship. Cole had no reason to be jealous of the ease with which the two men spoke. He really didn't know Owen all that well, and while he had a certain amount of unrequited lust for the bartender, that amounted to nothing.

So why the hell did he want to punch Xander?

He forced his hand to relax. "I'm looking forward to buying some of your beer. I have to admit, I haven't tried it before now."

"Speaking of that." Xander narrowed his gaze at Owen. "Now that your old man isn't in charge of the bar, we need to talk about getting Steel Anvil on tap there. I want to expand out more in Toronto, and you're the natural first stop."

Cole didn't know if this had been a long-standing issue, or if there was more to it, but the second Xander mentioned the bar Owen stiffened.

"Dad didn't really get the whole microbrew thing. But you're right: it's long past due. I'll give you a call on Monday and we can have a chat." Owen turned to Cole and smiled. "We better get you upstairs before all the good stuff is gone. You need to get some of their Barking Beaver stout. Amazing stuff. It'll put hair on your chest."

Cole might be a bit thick when it came to romance, but he knew when someone wanted him to get them out of an awkward situation. "Sounds good. I want some of that IPA as well."

They left the brewery with arms full of paper bags containing what Cole hoped was good beer. Xander had thrown in a Steel Anvil

Brewery T-shirt on their way out the door. Cole doubted he'd ever have an occasion to wear the gray shirt with the cartoon beaver holding a hammer over an anvil, but it was free. He liked free.

It had started snowing while they'd been inside. The sidewalk was slick and slushy, making the walk to the car challenging. Owen was being surprisingly quiet, and Cole didn't have a clue what was wrong.

"I'm parked over here." He led the way to his car, walking around to the trunk. "Thanks for today. I never realized how much of a process there was to making beer. Makes me appreciate it that much more."

He'd placed the bags into the trunk and slammed it shut when Owen spun him around and pressed his ass against the car. He opened his mouth to complain about the inevitable salt stains this would leave on his coat and pants, but the words died on his tongue.

Snow clung to the tips of Owen's hair and eyelashes. His cheeks had already reddened from the cold and his brown eyes were fixed on Cole's. Owen flexed his hands, and despite the thickness of his coat, Cole could feel the pressure on his arm.

"Owen?"

"I promised myself I wouldn't take advantage of you." He licked his lips, and his gaze dropped for a moment. "While you've been coming into the bar for a while now, it's not like I know you. It's wrong and messed up that I want nothing more than to strip you naked and fuck you into next week."

"I want to fuck you too." A rush of desire and surprise mixed in Cole's body. His previously hard cock took that opportunity to make itself known again. Yes, sex was an excellent idea. "This doesn't have to mean anything. No commitments."

"Sex as a way to forget?" Owen cocked his eyebrow. "It's a terrible idea."

"I know." It was strange, he'd had an almost identical conversation with Steven when they'd first gotten together. *Today the part of Steven will be played by Cole.* "I don't care. I want to feel something other than this pain in my chest that doesn't want to go away. I'm tired of closing my eyes and seeing Steven at the airport, the look on his face as . . . I just need something tangible. You are very tangible."

Owen growled. "I'm going to kiss you. Then I'm going to get in your car and we're going to your place. Or my place. Whichever is closer."

"My condo is by the bar."

"I live above the bar."

"What are we going to do about your car?"

"I live above a bar. I can walk home later and get my car tomorrow."

With each heartbeat, Owen drifted closer. His mouth hovered above Cole's for a moment before he leaned in and claimed him. Cole's breath hitched at the gentle contact, the soft slide of their lips, the hot touch of Owen's tongue. His pounding heart echoed in his ears, blocking out all other sounds. Owen slid his hand up and cupped Cole's cheek as he deepened the kiss.

Fuck.

He pushed Owen away. "Your place. Now."

CHAPTER SIX

Owen didn't remember much of their drive to the bar. If he'd been thinking, he would have driven himself home, or suggested they come together in the first place. He hadn't thought to ask Cole where he lived before inviting him out, which was a clear indication of his state of mind. And here they were now, going back to his apartment to fuck.

Cole was just as quiet as Owen was on the drive through Toronto traffic. Owen made sure to keep his hand on Cole's thigh, rubbing and squeezing, needing to feel the connection. This might not be more than sex for either of them, but having the best possible sex was high on the list of things he wanted to give him.

He needed this distraction as much as Cole did.

Seeing Xander normally didn't bring up much in the way of old feelings. They'd been friends longer than they'd been lovers. Xander would always hold a special place in Owen's heart, being the first man he'd ever slept with. But they'd been horrible as a couple, despite their mutual love of beer and bars. They'd argued more times than he could count about where their relationship was going, getting Steel Anvil into his dad's bar, and hockey, amongst other things. Things were better when they could walk away from one another and not have to worry about who would sleep on the couch.

He hadn't had a serious relationship with a man since Xander, only the occasional partner. Owen didn't know why, but he'd just assumed that while he enjoyed fucking a man, he wasn't wired to get into a long-term relationship with one. But seeing Xander standing beside Cole did strange things to him. Especially when he caught Xander checking out Cole's ass. That had sent an irrational rage whipping through him that wouldn't have ended well.

"Almost there." Cole slid his hand over where Owen was gripping him.

Owen didn't normally invite people to his place for sex. It was his safe haven, the spot that he'd claimed as soon as he'd been able to afford a place of his own. His dad had bought the building ten years earlier, but Owen insisted on paying rent regardless. Now that he was running the bar full-time, he went rent-free as part of his payment.

He wanted to see Cole there. Wanted to push him against the wall, rip his shirt off so he could sate his curiosity about the other man's chest. He wanted to see him spread out on the middle of his bed, moaning and begging for Owen to suck him off, to fuck him.

Shit, he couldn't wait.

At the next red light, he slid his hand up Cole's thigh and cupped his cock through his jeans.

"Fuck." Cole bucked up, his body restrained by the seat belt. "What the hell?"

"The things I want to do to you." He gave the shaft another squeeze. "I've been hard since we left the brewery. I have this porn movie of things . . . positions and noises, playing in my head."

"Stop." Cole groaned. "Please, I need to drive."

"You can't multitask?"

"Not with your hand on my groin like that."

Owen had always had a bit of an evil streak in him. Without looking, he found Cole's zipper and began to tug.

Cole swallowed. "What are you doing?"

"Helping you improve your multitasking abilities."

"You're going to cause an accident."

"We're almost there."

"Oh my God." Cole's breathing caught. "We're going to die. I'm going to die in a car accident with my cock out."

His fingers finally found what he was looking for: the soft brush of cotton and the hard press of flesh. There wasn't much room for him to move, so he simply flexed his fingers around the head of Cole's cock.

"I hate you," Cole muttered through his clenched teeth.

"I promise to make it up to you." Owen pushed his fingers down as low as they'd go, trying to tease Cole's balls. "You'll love it."

They turned into the parking garage to Cole's condo—God, he really was close to the bar—and Owen held back until they pulled into a parking spot. The second Cole threw the car into park, Owen released their seat belts, leaned over, and yanked down Cole's underwear as far as he could manage.

"You have a nice cock." He sucked the tip into his mouth.

It had been a long time since he'd given head, but there were certain things a person didn't forget how to do. Sucking cock was one of them. The angle was awkward, the restriction of the car and Cole's clothing frustrating, but he didn't care. Now that he had his mind set on giving a blowjob, nothing was going to stop him. Careful not to catch Cole with his teeth, he began to bob up and down, teasing every bit of skin that he could touch.

Cole's hand found its way to the back of Owen's head. Tentative at first, he stroked his hair. The harder Owen sucked him, the more aggressive Cole's caresses became. Finally, he tugged on the short strands, encouraging him. "Harder."

He was only happy to oblige.

The smell of Cole's arousal filled his nose and made his mouth water. Using the tip of his tongue, he teased the nerve bundle of Cole's cock. He wanted to be able to play with his balls without restriction, tug on them until Cole was begging for release, but that would require stopping, moving, things that he didn't want to do. Not yet. He continued to work Cole's shaft, licking what little of the skin he could see. Cole began to set a steady pace with his hand. Up and down, nice and slow, just the way Owen liked to go.

"I can't come like this," Cole groaned. "Let's go in."

"No." He nipped gently at his cockhead.

"Come on. My place is just upstairs."

"No."

"Owen, *please*. I need you to fuck me. Hard. I need to feel something, something raw."

Oh. That sounded good. Careful not to trap Cole's cock with the elastic of his underwear, Owen sat up. "I hope to God you have condoms."

Cole's face was flushed and his breathing was coming in shallow puffs. "A whole box. Unopened."

That was all Owen needed to hear. He was up and out of the car before he gave himself time to reconsider. Cole took a minute longer, no doubt needing to recover. Good to know that he hadn't lost his touch.

Owen patted the trunk of the car. He might as well bring the beer up. They'd hopefully need it to quench their thirst once they were done. Cole popped it before he staggered out of the car.

"I'll carry this." Owen winked at him. "You don't look too steady on your feet."

"I hate you." He adjusted the front of his pants, doing his best to shove his cock in safely.

"No, you don't. Because in ten minutes I'm going to have you stripped naked and your cock down my throat so far I'll gag. Then if you're lucky, I'll fuck you senseless."

Cole groaned, grabbed him by the arm, and dragged him to the elevator.

The reality was it took closer to five minutes for them to wait for the slow elevator and make their way through the building to Cole's condo. In any other situation, Owen would have taken the opportunity to admire the amenities. It was certainly a nicer place than what Owen could afford. But he didn't give a shit about building security, the nice foyer, or the smell of chlorine from what must have been a pool. All that mattered was getting naked, quickly.

Cole fumbled with his keys, needing two attempts before he could slide them into the lock. The second they crossed the threshold, Owen set the beer on the floor, and tore his coat off as he kicked free of his boots. Cole mirrored his actions, and within moments he had Owen pressed against the wall, his mouth covering his. *Yes*, this was what he'd wanted, what had been missing from his life. The bar and his dad's health had consumed him for so long he'd forgotten what it was like to simply let go and live his life. Cole had his own demons to exorcise. Owen couldn't imagine why Cole's boyfriend had left him, but he was more than happy to let himself be used if it would help.

Wrapping his arms around Cole, he flipped them so the other man was now pressed against the wall and he was in a position to do what he'd promised. Placing a final kiss on Cole's lips, he slipped to his knees and quickly worked the front of Cole's jeans open. After all, he was a man of his word. Not being as careful as he should, he shoved the jeans down until they caught on Cole's thighs, before leaning in and capturing his cock in his mouth.

"Yes." Cole's hands cupped his face, his thumbs digging into Owen's jaw. "Fuck."

His little preview in the car hadn't prepared him for the beautiful package that was Cole's cock. Long but not too thick, and curved ever so slightly to the left. Owen took as much of it as he could until the head pressed against the back of his throat. His mouth watered in response, and he was forced to pull back so he could swallow.

"I could suck you all day." He dove back in, not taking as much so he could increase the suction. He teased the nerve bundle with the tip of his tongue at the same time he tugged on Cole's balls.

"You're . . ." Cole swallowed and tightened his hold on Owen's face. "I'm going to come. Stop."

There were two things he could do here: let Cole come, or stop and fuck him. They'd both wanted sex, he even knew Cole had condoms. But the microscopic part of his brain that was rational and still thinking knew that sex with a man he didn't know very well, and who was suffering from a broken heart, was probably on the universal list of shitty things to do to a person. Owen was many things, but he didn't like to think of himself as *that guy*.

He pulled back and looked up at Cole. His face was flushed red and his eyes were barely open. He was clenching his teeth, which forced the little muscle in his jaw to jump and twitch. Clearly, he was as close to the edge as he'd said he was. It would take nothing for Owen to push him over. To hear him cry out with pleasure.

Owen kept eye contact as he leaned in and gently licked the tip of Cole's cock. "I've changed my mind."

Cole's eyes bugged open. "What?"

"Not that. I'm going to suck your brains out your dick. But I'm not going to fuck you."

"Why not?" Cole's thighs began to quiver as Owen stroked him. "I'm . . . condoms . . ."

Owen's cock was also protesting in the confines of his jeans. *What do you mean no sex? Bad human. I will make you pay.* He pushed down on his dick as he licked along the length of Cole's.

"You're still grieving. I can't take advantage."

"You're not." Cole banged his head against the wall. "You're so not."

"I would be, and I can't." Another long swipe of his tongue from Cole's balls to his head. "But I'm not an asshole. I'm going to suck every last drop of cum from you. Consider it an early Christmas present."

That was all the talking he could manage. Closing his eyes, he focused on giving Cole the most pleasure he could. Long licks were exchanged for gentle nips. The scent of Cole's arousal was embedding in his head. He ran his hands along Cole's thighs and up until his fingers embedded into Cole's pubic hair. The wiry strands caught his calluses as he teased the pale skin. Heat and musk, moans and sighs, he cherished everything that was Cole.

He wanted to stretch things out as long as possible, but knew given his teasing at the brewery and his fondling in the car, there was little chance Cole would last much longer. The man deserved some pleasure after the shitty few days he'd gone through. Owen set a steady pace, using what he hoped was enough suction to finish Cole off. Adding his hand, he pumped Cole's cock and moaned as the bitter tang of pre-cum burst across his tongue.

"Yes," Cole hissed. His legs shook violently, and Owen knew it was only a matter of moments now.

Cole tightened his hold on Owen's face half a second before he cried out, and cum filled Owen's mouth. He didn't stop moving, sucking, doing everything he could to pull every bit of pleasure from Cole. Lust hit him hard, and he knew he'd have to do something to take care of his own raging hard-on before he left.

Shit, why did he say no sex? *Idiot.*

Finally, Cole's orgasm waned and he released Owen. With his legs protesting from the awkward position, Owen fell back onto his ass. Cum was sticky on his lips, and he couldn't help but lick it clean. For his part, Cole looked as though someone had ripped his soul from his body and all that remained was a blissed-out hull that wore a stupid grin.

Dude, you still got it. He gave himself a mental high five.

Cole slid to the floor, his legs knocking against Owen's. "You're hard."

"I am." He fumbled with his fly. "I'm going to jerk off. Hope you don't mind."

Cole didn't say anything, but he didn't look away either. Owen yanked up his shirt, wishing he'd had the foresight to wear something without buttons. Cock in his hand, he kept his gaze on Cole. He hadn't done something like this before. Jerking off was always a private thing, something that was more out of necessity than anything else. The thought of getting off with someone watching was surprisingly arousing.

He licked his palm, getting it wet before he started with an easy stroke. Nice and steady, the way he'd do if he was alone. The sounds his body made were obscene and added to the surrealism of the situation. Wet flesh being worked, stuttered breath, mixed with his uncontrollable gasps. His skin was superheated and his muscles spasmed as his orgasm inched closer.

He tried to ignore Cole, simply let his mind wander to the places it would normally go when he did this. It didn't stay there long though, as he became hyperaware of the man watching him get off. Cole's reactions to his masturbation became his focus. The other man's gaze flitted from his cock to his stomach and back to his hand. His mouth had fallen open, and his tongue darted out to moisten his lips.

"Do you have any idea what you look like?" Cole rolled his head to the side, but still remained pressed to the wall. "You have a perfect cock. Thick the way I like it. It would take you a while to get me ready to take you. When I was ready, you'd stretch my ass so wide. I'd feel you for days later."

Owen groaned and let his eyes slip closed.

"Your head is so red right now. I bet it would be hot in my mouth. Your cum would be hot on my tongue. I bet it wouldn't take more than a few seconds for me to suck you off."

It took less than that. With the mental image of Cole giving him head, Owen came hard. His orgasm rolled through him, shaking him to his core. Cum spilled across his fist and shot in a wet line across his stomach. His hips lifted off the floor as he thrust into his fist one final time, before collapsing into a boneless heap. A pair of shoes dug into his back, but he didn't give a shit.

He couldn't hear much beyond the pounding of his heart in his ears for several minutes. Hell, he hadn't noticed that Cole had gotten up until a warm facecloth landed on his stomach. He forced his eyes open to see Cole standing over him, a smirk on his face.

"We're doing twelve days of this?"

Owen chuckled. "I don't know if I'll survive." It only took him a minute to clean up and fix his clothing.

"Me either."

Now that the whole uncontrollable-need-to-come moment had passed, Owen couldn't shake his awkwardness. Shit, he hadn't even gotten fully into Cole's condo. The narrow hallway opened up into what looked like a living room of sorts. Not that he could see much of it from where he was. Yeah, this wasn't awkward at all.

He folded the facecloth so Cole wouldn't get anything on him and handed it back. "Thanks. And sorry for this."

"For sucking my brains out of my dick?" Cole grinned, the first genuine smile he'd given him since he'd walked into the bar over a week ago. "I'll forgive you this time. Just try to make sure it doesn't happen again."

"I'll do my best." He didn't normally do this *weirdness* with a partner. It was normally all about the sex, thanks so much, and have a great night. "I better leave you be." He found his coat draped over their beer purchases and slipped it on.

"Owen." Cole reached out and stopped him with the gentlest of touches. "Thank you. For everything. Today was good. I feel a bit more like myself again."

With those few words, all of his trepidation melted away. "You're welcome."

They hugged, more of a friendly gesture than anything romantically inclined. Cole stepped back and opened the door. "I'll see you soon."

Owen wouldn't admit it out loud, but it wouldn't be soon enough. "Good night."

The snow had started coming down in earnest by the time he'd reached the street. With his collar pulled up and his hands shoved into his pockets, he enjoyed the short walk to the bar. For the first time in ages, he was stress-free. Spending the day with Cole had done wonders for taking his mind off his dad and the bar. A much-needed break.

He was about to unlock the outside side door and head up to his place when his phone buzzed. There was a message from Cole.

I could use some help getting a Christmas tree tomorrow. Are you game?

He grinned and texted his affirmative. It seemed that helping Cole was going to be easier than he'd first thought. Now all he had to do was try to keep it in his pants.

CHAPTER
SEVEN

There were many things Cole felt guilty about, but Owen giving him one of the best blowjobs of his life certainly wasn't one of them. The fact that Cole had been willing to have sex but Owen had declined only served to increase Cole's obsession with the bartender.

Good-looking, successful, talented, *and* noble.

Before this week, Cole assumed men like Owen were little more than the equivalent of gay unicorns.

Sexy gay unicorns with big, thick horns.

"Jesus." He shook his head and finished his coffee.

He'd offered to drive Owen back to the microbrewery so he could pick up his car. Owen was going to follow behind him to the small tree lot outside of Toronto where Cole and his family always bought their firs.

Never in Cole's life had he been this excited about buying a Christmas tree, and they'd been doing this since he was five. His family had always made the holidays a big deal growing up. There were certain traditions that signified that the special time of year had arrived, ones that would feel wrong to omit. His mom always spent time decorating the tree after he and his sister took great pains to pick out the perfect one. After, they'd all enjoy some warm eggnog, and when he got older some with a bit of whiskey in it.

Good times.

He assumed that the missing decorations was the reason this year had felt off. When he'd decided to take Steven away over Christmas, he hadn't bothered setting anything up. His mom had been especially disappointed that not only was she *not* going to finally meet Steven, she was also going to miss out on Cole being home. He'd suggested to Steven that they go over to his parents' place before their trip, but the timing had never worked out.

Now he couldn't help but wonder if Steven had been trying to avoid meeting the family.

He'd had a fleeting thought to invite Steven along on the family Christmas tree hunt this year, a chance for them all to meet, but it hadn't felt quite right. This was a personal tradition, and their relationship had been too new. Going without him hadn't been fun either. Next year, he'd promised himself that he'd bring Steven. Not that it would happen now.

The wind had picked up at the tree lot, making his decision to get out of the car feel foolish. Owen had only been a short distance behind him, so he wasn't expecting to be out there long. He stamped his feet and pulled his scarf a bit tighter. He'd already claimed his marker that would indicate which tree he wanted the lot manager to cut down. He had everything he needed. No excuses to move or wander, and no desire to go anywhere without Owen.

He didn't want to examine that thought even a little.

Finally, Owen's Hyundai turned the corner and zipped up the short snow-packed road, coming to a stop beside him. Relief washed through him as he watched Owen fumbling with something before he pushed his door open.

"I thought I'd lost you." He walked over to Owen's door, surprised when a hot coffee was shoved into his hands. "Bless you."

That grin of Owen's did more to melt the cold in his chest than the heat from the coffee. "I saw a little place before the turn. I figured we could use it. It's too frigging cold."

Cole was still surprised by Owen's height, especially when he didn't give much in the way of personal space and crowded against him. Owen bumped into him with a smile that told him the action was far from accidental. "So, Christmas trees? A real one?"

Yes, better to focus on the matter at hand and not relive memories of Owen's talented tongue teasing his cock. "Umm, yeah. I figured I better get one to brighten up my condo. While Steven has ruined my plans for the next week, I decided I wouldn't let him ruin everything."

"Good idea. And why don't you buy an artificial one?" Cole's horror at the suggestion must have shown on his face, as Owen laughed. "Sorry I asked."

"Simple answer: my mother would disown me."

"Gotcha." Owen sipped his coffee and looked around the small lot. "One small problem to your plan."

Rather than the abundance of trees Cole was used to seeing, the few trees that remained were either little or misshapen. Between the rejects were a series of stumps where trees had been cut. "I've never waited this long to get one before. I've checked in with the lot owner. Once we tag the tree we want, we can get him from the office and he'll cut it for us."

"You mean I won't be able to show you my manliness by chopping down a tree?" Owen's pout was cute and fleeting. "Fine. We better get looking before any more stragglers show up. So what kind are you looking for?" Owen stepped into him again, bumping their shoulders. "I didn't even see your living room so I have no idea on size and stuff."

Cole was thankful for the cold, because the memory of Owen on his knees got him flustered. "I don't like anything too big." *Just bartenders.* "Around six feet tall is good." *And six inches long.*

It was strange walking through the sparse rows with Owen. For all the hesitations he'd felt about bringing Steven here, none of those reservations crossed his mind now. Weird.

"Oh, this looks good." Owen bounded down a row that possessed more stumps than trees. "It's only a little crooked."

"That's . . . pathetic."

Owen grinned. "It's a little thin, but nothing that can't be covered up. How much garland do you have?"

The branches looked as though someone had grabbed hold and yanked half of the needles off. "I don't think even Charlie Brown would take that one home."

"Less for you to clean up in the end." Owen walked around it, peering through the branches. "I'm sure all we need to do is look around and . . . Oh."

Cole frowned and came over. "Oh what?"

The second he stepped into the space between the trees, Owen pulled him by the shoulders until their chests were flush. *He's going to kiss me.* His lips parted and his eyes threatened to close, until he realized Owen wasn't actually looking at him. The next moment he was spun around and facing away from Owen.

"That one." Owen's voice was soft in his ear. The nearness made him shiver and he wanted to press his head against the side of Owen's. "It's perfect."

What?

He blinked when he realized that Owen was talking about a tree. "I don't . . ."

Then he saw it.

Shorter than the one Owen initially identified, this tree was hidden from the path by two crooked ones. If they hadn't been standing in that exact spot, neither of them could have seen it. The branches were full and the trunk straight, even if it wasn't overly tall. It would fit flawlessly into the corner of his living room by the window and was just big enough to support all of his decorations. And Owen had found it.

"That really is perfect."

That was the natural cue for him to step forward and claim his tree. It would mean stepping away from Owen's body, the solid mass currently pressed to his back. It would also mean moving away from the brush of warm breath against his cheek, leaving behind their little secluded spot that wrapped them in pine scent and sunshine.

"Cole?" He heard Owen swallow.

"Yeah?" What the hell was the matter with him? They were here to get a tree, not rub against one another like two teenagers in heat.

"Is this a rebound thing?"

"I think so." There was no point in lying to Owen or to himself.

"But once we bring your tree back to your place and put it up, we can have sex? I'm not taking advantage of you, or leading you on?"

"Yes to sex. No to taking advantage."

"This doesn't make me an asshole? Because I don't want you to think of me that way. I also had bowling on my list of things to distract you."

Cole burst out laughing as he turned. "Bowling?"

Owen shrugged. "I like to bowl. Playing with balls. Sex works too."

Without caring about who would see, Cole leaned in and placed a soft kiss to Owen's cold lips. "Let's get my tree and head back to my place. We can have sex. I want to have sex."

The look on Owen's face couldn't have been any more perfect if he'd been told he'd won the lottery. Given what little about him Cole knew, maybe that's exactly how it was. Not wanting to stop himself, he leaned in and kissed Owen again. Unlike the brush of cold lips before, he closed his eyes and kissed him deep. They weren't touching, not really possible given the layers of clothing between them. But Cole felt more from that single connection—more passion, *lust*—than he had in his entire time with Steven.

The brush of Owen's tongue against his pulled a moan from him. He wrapped his arms around Owen, desperately wanting to feel the weight of him against his chest. The kiss deepened, and his awareness narrowed to the man before him. The quiet strength, the feel that Owen would make everything all right. It didn't matter that they were practically strangers. This wasn't about a relationship. It was sex. It was a rebound, but they both had their eyes wide open.

Nothing bad would come from this.

"Oh look, there are some more trees down here."

Cole pulled back with a gasp. "Shit."

Owen snatched the marker from his hands and raced over to the tree. "This one's taken!"

The next moment happened as though the world had hit the slow-motion button. Owen running toward his tree, his arm outstretched as he went. The giggles, then gasps of children as Owen's boot caught on a tree stump, which sent him flying through the air, head-first into his tree. The soul-crushing sounds of the impact and the cracking of breaking branches.

The whole time Cole could only watch as Owen's body landed awkwardly on the ground. As suddenly as everything slowed, the world raced forward again, freeing him from his stunned state. "Shit! Owen!"

He raced over to where Owen was, joined by the family of five that had tried to take his tree. The woman nudged her way past her kids and joined Cole on the ground. "I'm a paramedic."

Owen groaned as a trail of blood dripped down the side of his face. "Tagged it." Then he smiled at the group staring down at him.

"Hey, what's your name?" The woman snapped her fingers in front of Owen's face before pulling a cloth from her pocket and pressing it to his wound. "Pay attention."

"This is Cole's tree."

"Yes, we got that. What's your name?"

"Owen."

"Day of the week?"

"Sunday."

"Month?"

"December."

"Who's this?" She poked Cole's shoulder.

"Cole. I'm his rebound guy." Owen grinned as the kids giggled.

The woman rolled her eyes. "Good for you. Okay, Owen, you need stitches and should be checked out for a concussion." She turned to Cole. "He's probably fine, but I'd let a doctor make that call. Do you need help getting him out of here? I can call an ambulance."

Any remaining thoughts of hot sex were instantly replaced with route calculations to the nearest hospital. "No, we'll be fine. I'll drive him."

Another pout from Owen. "That means I have to leave my car again."

"It will survive."

It took a minute to get him to his feet, but Owen managed and seemed to enjoy using Cole as a crutch. He also wouldn't go anywhere until the family took their leave and went in search of a different tree. He leaned against Cole and whispered, "I saw the husband eyeing your fir."

Dear God. "I don't think he was going to take it. You've already bled all over it."

"You never know. We need to get this thing cut down and put on your car."

"The tree can wait. I want a doctor to take a look at you."

Owen stepped away. "No."

"What? You need to get to a hospital. Stitches, remember? Concussion?"

Owen shook his head, wincing at the motion. "That can wait. We are going to get this tree cut, on your car, and back to your place. If the bleeding hasn't stopped by then, I will go to the hospital. But not before. You've had too many things happen to you this year. Too many people putting their needs before yours. I'm not going to be another one on that list." Owen reached out and secured the tag on the tree. "Now let's bring this baby home."

Cole wasn't one to cry. It wasn't in his DNA, or something. But at some point in Owen's speech the tears filled his eyes and threatened to fall. No one had done something like this before. His parents relied on him now that they were older. His sister was always after him to help her fix things around her apartment. Hell, even Steven had wanted him to make things better. Cole was the fixer.

For the first time in his life, it was nice to have someone else willing to step into that role.

"Okay." He turned away so Owen wouldn't see the unshed tears. "We'll get the tree and bring it back. But we'll take your car. I can always get mine later."

"Deal." Owen winked at him. "We don't want to scratch up the Lexus."

"Always the gentleman. Come on, dumbass, let's find the lot owner before you pass out from blood loss."

As they walked toward the office, and despite the bitter wind, warmth bloomed in Cole's chest. If this was what a rebound romance could do for a person, no wonder people fell hard and fast. Typically they never ended well for either party, so he'd have to be extra careful to keep his emotions in check.

If he knew anything, it was that he'd never survive another broken heart.

CHAPTER EIGHT

It had taken Cole almost the entire trip back to Toronto to convince Owen to stop at the emergency room. Owen didn't want to admit it, but he probably wouldn't have gone if left to his own devices. He was stupid and stubborn and hated waiting at the hospital, especially this time of year. Too many flus, colds, and sick kids.

Thankfully, there wasn't a long wait and they got in quickly. He didn't appear to have a concussion, but he'd ended up with three stitches that finally stemmed the bleeding. Thank God for that because he didn't have the stomach for blood. The headache sucked though, and it was only made worse as they wrangled the tree into the elevator of Cole's building and dragged it down the hallway to his condo.

Still, he felt as though he'd won the day. He'd gotten a sexy scar out of the deal. A dating war wound that he could proudly show off.

Why yes, I did jump in front of a charming family to get a Christmas tree for a brokenhearted man. And I'd do it again! Of course you can totally take me out to dinner.

The thought of getting back out on the dating circuit was less than appealing these days. It was fun with Cole because he knew that the other man wasn't looking for anything serious. It was a bit of joy to help brighten his holiday and hopefully have some great sex in the meantime. Not that sex was on that afternoon's agenda, given the throbbing headache, the nasty head wound, and the unsightly bloodstains.

Too bad he'd cockblocked himself because of a fucking tree.

He sighed and looked around Cole's place as he guarded the tree. Cole had disappeared into a spare room and was rummaging around looking for the tree stand and his decorations.

"I found the box. One second."

He bit his tongue to stop from making any inappropriate *box* jokes. "All good. I'm just protecting the tree and gawking at your books."

"Dude, you don't have to stand there. Sit down and rest. Safe to say you've earned the break."

"I'm fine." He really wasn't, but Cole didn't need any more guilt added on. The ride back had consisted of them making sure the tree didn't blow off and Cole asking if he was okay. The pain in his head pulsed again. "But I'll sit if it makes you feel better."

"It will."

Well then, if it made *Cole* feel better.

The couch held a number of big cushions that hugged his body as he got comfortable. The backrest was soft and inviting, yielding to his head and neck as he stretched out. Oh this was good, it fit him in a way most furniture didn't. He'd close his eyes for a moment, just until Cole came out with the things, and then he'd help with the decorations . . .

"Owen?"

He jumped and nearly bashed his face against Cole's. "Shit. What's wrong?"

"Nothing. You fell asleep."

Blinking, he looked around and saw that Cole had not only found the box of decorations, but he'd put the tree in the stand and had already strung lights on it. "How long was I out?"

"Half an hour or so." Cole stepped back, his hands on his hips. "I would have let you sleep longer, but your phone was ringing in your coat. Thought it might be important."

The only people who normally called his cell number were his parents and Jane from the bar. "I better check that."

"Stay there, I'll grab it." Before he could protest, Cole was already gone.

"The tree looks good." It was nice to know that his sexual sacrifice had been worth it.

"It's the best one I've ever had. Here you go."

The message light was flashing, and Jane's number was in the list. "This is work. I better check it."

Cole stepped away and continued decorating the tree as Owen typed in his password. The second he heard Jane's voice he knew there was a problem.

"Hey, boss. Sorry to bug you on your day off but we have a . . . situation. Your dad is here and . . . I can't get a hold of your mom. If you can come in as soon as you're able, that would be good. Thanks."

The message hadn't finished playing and he was on his feet and moving toward the door.

"Owen?"

He stopped and spun around. "Cole. Damn it. I'm so sorry, but I have to head over to the bar. There's a problem."

"Anything I can help with?" Cole still held a small red Christmas bulb in his hand as he closed the distance between them. "You don't look very steady on your feet and I'm good at dealing with drunks now."

At the mention of the drunk, Owen's gaze flicked to the now-yellow bruise on Cole's face. The last thing he wanted to do was unload on him; Cole didn't need that after everything else he'd been dealing with. Owen certainly didn't want to inflict his dad on him, especially if he was in one of his moods. "I'll be good. It's a short walk and you have a tree to decorate."

Cole nodded and smiled. It didn't quite reach his eyes. "Be careful, then. And thank you for helping with the tree. It's perfect."

God, he didn't want to leave. It was strange how at ease he'd become in Cole's company. Stress he hadn't realized was weighing him down always dissipated the moment he saw Cole. The time they spent together was never long enough, and left him wanting more.

Ignoring the ache in his head, he kissed Cole hard. Like it had back at the tree lot, everything slotted into place for him. They fit together. He'd never had this level of comfort with another man before. It had always been about sex, hot and fast. The passion had been limited to physical attraction and nothing more.

With Cole, things were different.

Owen pulled back, knowing if he let the kiss go on too long he'd never leave the condo. "I'll give you a call later?"

"Looking forward to it."

The moment he left the safety of Cole's place, the urgency surrounding Jane's phone call and his father's presence at the bar hit him. Ignoring his head, he ran to the bar as quickly as he could manage on the slippery sidewalk. McGregor's Closed sign was still flipped around, but the door was unlocked. Jane and Moe would be setting up for the night, and wouldn't have unlocked it.

His dad had a key, though.

Opening the door, he was greeted with the sound of a glass smashing.

"How dare you try and give dirty dishes to my customers!"

Shit.

His dad was standing behind the bar, red-faced. Moe stood in the doorway to the back, arms stretched out as if to stop his dad from going back there. Jane was behind the bar with him, standing far closer to his dad than Owen would have liked.

Jason McGregor was normally an even-keeled man; even when Owen had gotten into trouble as a kid, he rarely lost his temper. But when he did, well, everyone ran for cover.

"Mr. McGregor, I promise you everything is clean." Jane's voice was shaky and she held both her hands up. "Look, Owen's here. I told you he was on his way. I know he'll be able to sort everything out."

"Dad, what's going on?" He slipped his coat off and set it over the back of a chair. "We're not open yet. We don't have your beer ready or anything."

"I'm not here for a beer." He looked at Owen, but his gaze didn't settle for long.

The closer Owen got to his dad, the easier it was to see how unhinged he was. His eyes were wide and the flush on his cheeks traveled down his neck. From this distance Owen was able to see that his dad was sweating.

"Jane, why don't you and Moe continue getting set up for tonight. Check to see if Ryan is in yet." He took her place behind the bar with his dad, giving her arm a squeeze as she went.

"Who's Ryan? And you shouldn't be opening the bar on Sunday. It's against God."

"Dad, you need to calm down."

"Don't you tell me what to do. I'm a grown man." His lips were pressed together in a solid line. "And you didn't answer me. Who is she talking about?"

This wasn't going to be easy. "Ryan is one of our cooks. He works on Sundays because he goes to school through the week."

"When I ran this place I never once opened the bar on a Sunday. Your mother would have forbidden it."

"We talked about this when I took over. We open late Sunday for the sports crowd. Hockey and football. We've been doing this for over a year now."

"They can damn well watch that shit at home."

"We already talked about this a long time ago. I can't change things now."

His father hadn't been pleased when Owen had suggested that they open the bar for a little while on Sundays, but they'd talked about it and he'd understood that the extra money the food and beer sales brought in would help with their bottom line. Owen had worked hard to turn McGregor's into a destination, rather than an afterthought.

He thought everything had been fine.

"Dad, what's really wrong?" He came a bit closer and gently put a hand on his father's shoulder. "How can I help?"

His father opened his mouth, but nothing immediately came out. It was strange, but for a moment his dad looked lost, confused, and for the first time since he'd agreed to let Owen take over the bar, unsure of himself.

"I want the bar back."

Owen let his hand drop. "What?"

"I don't like how you're running things. You're going to damage the reputation of McGregor's. I've worked too hard to watch you destroy this."

His words were a silent knife to Owen's chest. "What's brought this on? You've seen the financials. We've been doing well, especially leading up to the holidays."

"Faked."

"Dad, they're not faked—"

"How would you know? You're running off with some . . . some queer and—"

"Hey!" In all his years, he'd never heard his father say anything derogatory about anyone. *The fuck was going on?* "Are you trying to piss me off? Because you're succeeding. I've been running the bar for two years now, and we've been doing great. My personal life has nothing to do with it. Mom would be ashamed of you if she heard you use that word."

"Fine. You don't want me here, I'll go. Move." He pushed by Owen, shoved past several chairs, and stomped out the door.

Owen was paralyzed. That wasn't his father. The fear and hate coming from him hadn't been something Owen had seen from his old man ever in his life. It was as though an alien had taken up residence inside the kind, generous man and didn't know how to behave.

He felt rather than saw Jane standing in the doorway. "I don't know your dad well, but there was something wrong with him."

"I know. That's not . . . that's not how he acts." He pulled out his phone and called his mom. "Hey."

"Owen? I was at the market with Jessica. Drove her to get her Christmas turkey. I got back and your father was gone."

"He was here." His voice cracked, the anger and fear threatening to break free.

"What's wrong?"

"I was going to ask you the same thing." This wasn't his mom's fault, but she had to know that something was going on. "He was angry, wanted to take control of the bar again. Saying things . . . He wasn't acting like himself."

"Oh."

"Oh? That's all you have to say? What's wrong with him?"

"I thought it was just me. That I was the one upsetting him."

It was typical of her not to let him know there was a problem until things were bad. He hadn't known his dad was having health issues until after he ended up in the hospital with a stroke. "How long has he been acting like this?"

"A few months now." Her voice had gone soft, and he knew she was trying not to cry.

"Mom, how long?"

"I started noticing that he wasn't right about six months ago."

"Jesus. Why didn't you say anything?"

"You'd taken over the bar. You were running yourself ragged trying to get it cleaned up and profitable again. You'd taken on that load, and I was looking after him. You didn't need anything else to worry about."

He leaned against the bar and let his head fall forward. "Are you okay?"

"I am."

"Mom?"

"Honestly, I am. Though it's been a bit stressful this last little while. He's been getting more irritable than I've ever seen."

"He needs to see his doctor."

"I've tried but he won't go."

"Then we make him."

She sighed. "I'm more worried about where he is right now. You said he left?"

"He stormed out of here angry. I'm not sure where he went, but it couldn't be far."

"Probably to see Stuart. I'll call to give him some warning and ask that he drive him home."

When he hung up with his mom, Owen couldn't shake the weight that had settled on him. This was worse than the stroke. Then he had known what was wrong and what course of action he could take to make things right. Quitting his job and taking over the bar made sense. Now . . . he didn't know where to start.

That wasn't true. He'd promised his dad that he'd make sure McGregor's would always be up and running. He wasn't about to let that change now.

Standing, he turned to see Jane still hovering by the entrance. It was three o'clock and the bar opened in an hour. "Is Ryan here?"

"Yeah, he slipped in the back a while ago. Owen, what happened to your head?"

"Long story, but I'm fine. Let's help Ryan prep and get set up. We've got a bar to open."

CHAPTER NINE

ole sat in the spot where Owen had been hours earlier and stared at his fully decorated Christmas tree. It really had been the perfect one for him, its size and shape fitting into his condo as though it had taken root and grown there. Owen had found it, had bled for it, and had dragged it back for him.

It was very caveman in a way.

He liked that.

What he didn't like was being alone. It gave him time to think, which was both good and bad. The last few days hanging out with Owen had eased his broken heart. His anger had dissipated and he was finally able to clear his mind and look at the whole Steven situation somewhat rationally. Well, as rationally as he could when he had a box of his ex's stuff sitting at his feet.

He had this random collection—a toothbrush, Steven's DJ Tiësto shirt, his copy of *To Kill a Mockingbird*, some other random odds and ends—and he didn't know where to send them. He'd texted Steven to see if he wanted to come get his things, only to be told that he'd gone to Montreal for a trip with . . . whatever the hell his name was.

Adam. Right.

Cole didn't know any of Steven's family; he'd never met them. They'd only hung out with Steven's friends a few times. He'd gotten the impression that they weren't big fans of his. He'd never minded when Steven had gone out with them and he'd stayed behind. The thought of taking the box to any of them, to see the look of *oh thank*

God Steven came to his senses, was too much. It served as a reminder that things would never have worked between them.

Deep down, he had probably always known that. It had nothing to do with the difference in their ages or incomes, and everything to do with their personalities. Steven was an extrovert to the *n*th degree. He liked to party, dance, hit the clubs, all the things Cole didn't enjoy. Bars like McGregor's had always been more Cole's speed. The game or fight on the television, people to talk to about what was happening if he wanted. Or the option to simply sit and be left alone if that's what he preferred.

Thinking about McGregor's meant his mind made its way around to Owen. The idea of becoming entwined with the bartender was a fantasy come true. He was an attractive man with a mouth that could turn a straight man gay. And if he hadn't had the opportunity to feel the slide of Owen's cock into him, well, that was something he could hopefully look forward to.

But if Cole knew one thing about himself, it was that he had a tendency to jump from the frying pan into the fire. While he might be coming to realize that his relationship with Steven had been doomed from the beginning, that didn't mean getting into something with Owen would necessarily work either, no matter how different Owen and Steven were. If he came out of this breakup learning nothing else, it was that rebound romances were never, *ever* a good idea.

So he'd taken up residence in the spot where Owen had fallen asleep, sipping his eggnog and whiskey drink, staring at his Christmas tree.

Alone.

"Merry fucking Christmas."

Nope, he wouldn't sit here and feel sorry for himself. Picking up the remote, he turned on the television and flipped through the channels until he found a holiday movie. *It's a Wonderful Life* wasn't one of his favorites, but at least everything turned out for the best in the end. Jimmy Stewart walked around the screen talking to his angel as he tried to figure out his life. Cole wondered what his own guardian angel was up to. Probably escorting a few drunks to taxis, buying supper for a deserving family, or saving a kitten from a tree. Typical bartending stuff.

He lasted all of fifteen minutes before becoming overwhelmed with the saccharinity of the movie, and went in search of the Leafs game. Oh good, they were up in the second period. "That won't last long."

He was on his feet, swearing as the Rangers scored in the top of the third period to tie things up when his doorbell rang. He moved to answer it, his eyes glued on the screen as he walked backward. Opening the door, his attention snapped to a downtrodden Owen standing there. Not just exhausted, but looking emotionally beaten. Without knowing what was wrong, there was nothing he could do to fix it. But Owen didn't appear to be up for a lengthy conversation.

So he handed Owen his nearly full beer. "Rangers just tied it up."

"Fuckers."

And that was it. Owen kicked off his shoes and went toward the couch. Cole grabbed three beers because he knew they'd need more than the one before the game was over, and joined him.

It was a wonderful feeling knowing that they didn't have to say anything. Owen was upset, and he would talk about it when he was ready. Cole didn't feel the pressure to put his life on pause to hold his hand. He didn't need to push him to talk when he didn't want to. They were just two guys, having a beer and watching the game.

"Come on, ref!" Owen was leaning forward, his eyes fixed on the screen. "They jammed him up."

Cole's gaze darted from the screen to watch the muscles in Owen's neck move as he swallowed down his beer. He'd never had an obsession with a man's throat before. So weird.

"Yes, power play."

"Go, go, go!"

The Leafs scored with thirty seconds left in the period, bringing both men to their feet, cheering. Owen reached out and grabbed Cole's shoulder, a move that Cole now associated with him. "Hold them. Come on we need the win. Give me an early Christmas present."

Finally, the seconds ticked down and the buzzer screamed. Cole whooped and Owen laughed manically. He pulled Cole into a hug that squeezed the air from his lungs. "That was awesome."

Cole pressed his nose to Owen's neck and breathed in the scent of bar. Alcohol and sweat mixed in a pleasant way, and served to enhance the excitement racing through him. He relaxed against Owen and enjoyed being held. Owen eased his hold as they stood there. The embrace wasn't sexual—hell, Cole didn't think it was even about affection. It was a physical connection that they both seemed to need more than anything.

He turned his head so his cheek rested against Owen's shoulder. "Are you okay?"

"Not really."

"How's your head feeling?"

"It's the least of my worries."

"Is there anything I can do to help?"

Owen's chuckle vibrated through Cole's chest. "I can think of a few things, but this is nice."

Sex rarely solved problems, but what it did do was take a person's mind off things long enough to let them catch their breath. They'd been circling around one another long enough now that it didn't feel as though either of them was taking advantage. Lifting his head, he kissed Owen long and slow, enjoying every sensation. Their breathing synchronized as the kiss grew lazy. There wasn't pressure, a driving need to get off *right the hell now*. For the first time since Owen had proposed his little plan, Cole knew there'd be no interruptions or head wounds to get in the way.

Owen had on his bar T-shirt, the one he always wore when working. The cotton was soft beneath Cole's fingers as he let his hands roam along Owen's back. As nice as it was, he wanted to feel warm skin and hard muscles, not fabric. He took hold of the bottom of the shirt and tugged it up.

"Naked," he muttered in between kisses. "Now."

Owen yanked his shirt off and then reached for Cole's. "Great idea."

Finally, their naked chests pressed together. Owen had considerably more chest hair than he did, but Cole didn't mind. He liked the way the hairs caught and slid against each other when they kissed. He lost track of how long they stayed that way, half-naked and making out like teens. It didn't matter.

Owen peppered kisses down the side of his jaw until he reached his ear. "Bedroom."

Cole didn't wait for anything else. He grabbed Owen by the top of his jeans and pulled him down the hall into his bedroom. Normally, he'd worry about things being clean in there. It was one of his quirks that drove Steven a bit mental. With Owen though, the state of his room didn't matter. They were about to get messy so who cared if his bed was made?

"Condoms? You promised you had some." Owen pushed him so he fell flat on his back in the middle of the bed. "An unopened box, if I remember correctly."

Right. Important things.

He reached toward the nightstand where he kept his supply, but Owen stopped him from going far. Owen crawled up his body, placing kisses against his stomach and his chest. Cole tried not to move because it felt so fucking good. He didn't even mind when Owen kissed just below his armpit, a spot on his body that had never once entered into his mind as being erogenous.

Who knew?

Owen stretched out and yanked open the drawer. "I love a man who's prepared." A strip of condoms and his half-empty bottle of lube landed against Cole's side.

"I do my best."

When he reached for them, Owen stopped him. "I don't think we're ready for the main event. Not yet."

Foreplay had always been something that he enjoyed, but it was more or less the beginning of the pattern that things always fell into. No matter who he was with, it seemed to be the same: cock stroking, blowjob, condom, doggy-style, cleanup. The only variation was if he was on the top or bottom. He could tell from the look in Owen's eyes as he tossed the supplies toward the pillows that his methodical approach to sex was about to change.

Owen rose up on his knees and put his hands on his hips. "I'm going to take your pants off. Then I'm going to spend the next while exploring. Is there anything you're not into?"

Now there was a question he'd never been asked before. "I . . . don't think so?"

Owen cocked an eyebrow. "You don't sound certain."

"Up to this point, my sex life has been pretty vanilla."

"We'll have to expand your horizons." The grin Owen gave him was positively satanic.

"God, help me." He had grown to trust Owen. If nothing else, maybe he'd pick up a few new tricks. "Have at me."

There wasn't a whole lot of rational thinking beyond that moment.

He lifted his hips as Owen pulled his jeans and underwear free and tossed them on the floor. Rather than going right for his cock, Owen surprised him: he sat down, stretching his legs out alongside Cole's, picked up Cole's nearest foot and brought it to his mouth.

"You smell like soap." Owen pressed his nose to Cole's arch and breathed in deep. "You showered today."

"Right after I finished decorating the tree." Jesus, that felt odd. It also somehow made his cock twitch.

"Are you ticklish?" Owen ran his nose along the side of his foot, up toward his ankle bone.

"I don't think so." He squeezed the blankets and hoped that would stop him from coming right off the bed.

"Good. Don't kick me."

The next thing he knew, Owen licked along his arch and up to his ankle. He cried out, his body tensing at the slide of soft wet tongue. "Fuck."

"People don't realize how sensitive our feet are. We stand on them all day, abuse them. Blood can pool there, so it's important to help get it circulating." Owen shifted again, this time massaging Cole's foot with his strong hands. "I don't have a thing for feet, but I've learned over the years that people don't pay enough attention to their bodies. The more you relax, the more you enjoy things."

"Are you saying I'm tense?" Cole reached down and palmed his cock.

Owen chuckled and nipped at his foot. "Just a little."

He then proceeded to lick, bite, and kiss every inch of Cole's legs. There wasn't a spot free from Owen's attention. He'd find a mole or blemish and kiss it until Cole squirmed. He'd drag his fingers along Cole's body, massaging his muscles until he was equal parts relaxed and aroused. Goose bumps rose and his nipples hardened. He became aware of the way the sheets slid along his skin, the coolness of the air compared to the warmth of Owen against him. Every sensation intensified until he couldn't take any more.

"I can think of better things to do with your mouth." He pushed his hands into Owen's hair, careful to avoid the cut on his scalp, and tried to direct him toward his cock. "I'm going to explode."

"I don't know about that." Owen rolled away and stood. It was only then that Cole realized the other man was still half-dressed. Owen grinned as he made quick work of removing the last of his clothing. "Last time I remember doing all the work. Maybe it's time for a little reciprocation. If you're up for it?"

The sight of Owen's hard cock was all the motivation he needed. "Get on the bed."

Owen was a beautiful man. There was something captivating about his body, the way his muscles bulged and the way his chest hair covered his chest. He didn't mind that Owen was bi. He even understood the attraction to women on a cerebral level. But something about a man's body spoke to him and fascinated him in a way that a woman's never had. The smell of their arousal, the taste of their sweat. The sounds they'd make when aroused. Cole loved the beauty of the male body and all of the testosterone baggage that came along with it.

Rather than jump right to his goal, he positioned himself between Owen's legs and ran his hands up the insides. It was fun to be on this end of things, to be the one watching, observing. Owen closed his eyes, but that little smile of his was still there. He'd been right when he'd said that people didn't tend to relax. Cole had been so focused on what Owen was doing to him, he hadn't realized that Owen himself was a bundle of tension.

He took a mental step backward. It was only this morning that they'd gotten his tree. Owen had gotten hurt in a silly attempt to make sure Cole got exactly what he wanted. Then he'd had to rush off to deal with a problem at work. It had been a long and exhausting day for him, and Cole wanted to show Owen the same level of attention and affection that he'd given him. Yes, there'd be a blowjob, but first some time to explore.

Starting with Owen's left calf, Cole massaged the muscles of the leg, moving slowly upward until his fingers got dangerously close to Owen's tightened balls. When Cole shifted over to the right calf, Owen growled. "That's mean."

"You were the one who told me people needed to slow down and relax."

"I was also the one who said you should give me a blowjob." He peeked at Cole from one eye. "Still waiting on that."

"Don't be an ass." Still, he picked up the pace a bit. As much as he enjoyed teasing Owen, he didn't want to deny himself the prize for long.

As he reached the inside of Owen's right thigh, he leaned down on the bed so he could kiss the spot where his fingers had been just moments before. Owen's cock was straining straight up, and a bead of liquid had formed at the tip. He wanted to lick it off, finally know what the man who'd starred in many of his late-night fantasies tasted like.

That's what the old Cole would have done.

The new Cole, the man who'd learned that his feet and armpits were erogenous zones, he wanted to do something different. He wanted to find a way to repay Owen for his kindness and thank him for his creativity and lust for life.

To start with, he wanted to suck the other man's balls.

Leaning in, he licked from the base of Owen's balls all the way to the tip of his cock. The scent of his arousal was strong. Though he'd come from work, there was nothing offensive about his taste or smell. If anything, Cole wanted more.

Moving back down to his balls, Cole gently sucked one into his mouth. He teased the uneven skin with his tongue as he squeezed the insides of Owen's thighs with his hands. With his head where it was, Owen's moans were muffled to him, but he didn't care. He felt the way the other man's body trembled beneath his touch. Emboldened, he pushed Owen's thighs apart farther, leaving nothing hidden from his sight.

Then, on impulse, he did something he'd never done before. He closed his eyes and licked across Owen's hole up to his balls. Owen's body tensed quickly, lifting him off the bed. "Fuck!"

Cole pulled away so he could look at Owen. "Damn. I'm sorry. I don't know why I did that."

Owen burst out laughing. "It's fine. Just wasn't expecting it."

"Weird?" He'd never had anyone do that to him, but he'd seen enough porn to be curious. "I shouldn't have done that. I'm sorry."

"Cole, believe me when I say that a little rimming is the last thing that will send me running." Owen sat up and leaned forward to awkwardly kiss him. "More. Please. If you want."

Cole shoved Owen's chest, sending him back to the mattress. Okay, so this was different and a wee bit kinky. Getting back into position, he closed his eyes, held his breath, and flicked his tongue across Owen's puckered hole. Rather than his previous reaction, Owen spread his legs even wider and sighed.

"Fuck, that feels so good."

What little restraint Cole had disintegrated. He licked and sucked on any piece of skin he could get his mouth on. Reaching up, he took hold of Owen's cock and did his best to stroke it in time with his licks. It didn't take long for both of them to get beyond the point of reason. Owen grabbed him by the shoulders and pulled him up until they were lying chest to chest.

The kiss they shared was deep, manic. Cole blindly searched for the condoms, unwilling to break their contact. He fumbled for a moment before he found the cool foil.

He pressed the packet into Owen's palm and finally lifted up for air. "Fuck me."

There was no argument. He rolled onto his back as Owen got to his knees and slipped the condom on. The only thing he knew for certain was that there'd be no doggy-style tonight. He needed the intimacy of face-to-face. Owen must have read his mind, because he lubed up his fingers and pressed one into Cole's ass. When the second finger slipped in and Owen began to stretch him, Cole grew impatient. He didn't care if things hurt. He wanted Owen, wanted to be filled *right the hell now*. Owen was as impatient. He looked at Cole with an unspoken *Please can I now?* that he responded to with a single nod.

The press of Owen's cock into him was slow and steady. He relaxed; he couldn't do anything but take, accept. It had been a long time since he'd done this. Steven always preferred to be fucked, and he'd been happy to oblige. He'd missed this though. It was intense, personal, and exactly what he needed.

A trickle of sweat slipped down Owen's cheek as he began to thrust. He'd lowered himself so they were chest to chest again, which trapped Cole's cock between them. The new angle also allowed Owen to press deep into him, hitting his prostate on every other thrust. Cole clung to Owen's body and rode the rising pleasure until he knew he wouldn't hold out much longer.

"I'm not going to last." He sucked on Owen's ear lobe. "Make me come."

Owen seemed to be a man who enjoyed having a purpose. His thrusts became deliberate, and it was no time before Cole lost the ability to think. His body overrode his mind. His balls tightened as Owen's body rubbed against his cock. *Yes, almost there.*

"Harder."

Owen complied.

"Faster."

Owen increased his pace.

Cole's body shuddered, and he stopped breathing for a moment before he came. Then he sucked in as much air as he could manage, and screamed. Cum flooded between them, coating their bellies as Owen pounded his ass. Within seconds, Owen cried out as he came, his thrusts becoming irregular until he drove forward one final time. Finally, they both stopped moving, and Owen collapsed against him.

Cole had to swallow a few times before he could speak. "Wow."

Owen slid to the side, but didn't break contact. "Yeah."

They were both sweaty, covered in cum and lube, and grinning like fools. Cole would normally be up fetching a cloth from the bathroom to help them get cleaned. Instead, he reached down and drew a lazy eight on his belly. "So rimming."

Owen laughed. "You've never done that I take it?"

"Never given or received."

"Not that I'm complaining, but what prompted that?" Owen took his hand, lacing their fingers.

That was a good question. "I don't know. It just seemed like it was something you'd appreciate." It didn't matter that Owen was the first lover he'd had who seemed more than willing to be a bit adventurous.

Cole had never felt quite right bringing up some of the things he'd wanted to try with a partner before tonight.

"It was. Totally was." Owen kissed the back of his hand. "And if you have anything else you want to try, feel free to go ahead. I'm willing to do just about anything twice."

It was wonderful to know that with Owen, he was safe to explore, to have fun with sex. He'd never been in a relationship before where that had been the case.

Not that they were in a relationship.

Shit, he didn't want that.

Did he?

"Hey, you okay?" Owen rose up on his elbow. "You tensed."

He wasn't going to ruin things, not when they'd been going so perfectly. "It's fine. That was my brain kicking back in." He got up and kissed Owen softly on the lips. "I'm going to get some things to clean us up. And some eggnog with whiskey. Want some?"

"Sure. I could use a nightcap." Owen winked before stretching back out on the bed. "Be quick because I can't promise I won't doze."

Cole wanted to do as asked, but he found himself standing in the bathroom staring at himself in the mirror. He looked sated, happy almost. Owen had put that look of contentment on his face. Which was amazing, but it was also temporary.

This wasn't something that could last long-term. Owen was every bit as much a rebound relationship for him as he'd been for Steven. He needed to keep reminding himself of this, of his emotional distance from Owen. He owed it to the other man not to put him in the position that Cole currently found himself in. He was too good a person for that.

No, Cole wouldn't let things go too far. He owed it to *himself.*

There would be holiday events, hockey games, sex—hell, even bowling. But under no circumstances could he fall in love with Owen. None.

CHAPTER TEN

Owen's head pounded. It had been that way since he'd gotten up in the morning, a steady ache just behind his eyes. He wanted nothing more than to blame it on drinking too much, or even his head wound from what he now mentally referred to as The Tree Incident. Either would be an acceptable alternative.

This particular pain had everything to do with his father.

Two days after the blowup at the bar—and consequently after some of the best sex Owen had had in years—his dad called to apologize for his behavior.

"I don't like some of the changes you've made," he'd huffed into the phone receiver, and Owen didn't need to see or hear his mother standing beside his dad to know she was there. "But it's your bar now and I have to accept these things. I promise I won't get in your way again."

Owen thought that would be the end of the matter—but it still left the issue of his father's refusal to go to the doctor despite weeks of his mother's best efforts. That meant Owen had to come in as the big guns and force the issue. It also meant that a few hours after coming to an uneasy peace after the apology, he was now the one sitting in the doctor's office with his dad, who was less than impressed.

"I don't need to see the fucking doctor."

"Dad, language." He mouthed *Sorry* to a woman who was holding an unhappy toddler in her lap. At least she looked as though she could sympathize.

"There's nothing wrong with me. I don't know why you won't listen."

"You're not acting like yourself. Plus it will make Mom happy. You know what they say about happy wives."

"They leave you the hell alone."

Owen rolled his eyes. "I don't think that's how it goes, but close enough."

"Mr. McGregor?" The nurse who'd been working at the office for as long as Owen could remember looked directly at them. "Dr. Khan is ready to see you now."

"Do you want me to go in with you?"

His dad glared at him as he stood. "I'm not a child."

The pounding in Owen's head increased as he watched him walk away. *Wonderful.*

With time on his hands, he checked his phone for messages. The bar wouldn't be open yet, but that didn't mean he didn't have work to do. He answered a few emails before checking his texts. The second he saw Cole's number, he smiled.

I had a great time the other night. I got to thinking if you're free, maybe we could have another outing. I remember hearing something about bowling . . .

He really didn't want to be away from the bar at night, especially this close to the holidays. McGregor's would be packed with company parties, students celebrating the end of exams, and people who didn't want to be alone. It meant long days and nights for Owen.

Still, it wouldn't be too bad if he slipped out for a little while for a break. They could bowl a few rounds and then come back to the bar for a drink. Life wouldn't end if he took a bit of time for himself.

Hey. I think I can slip you in tonight between rounds. Meet me at the bar at 7? I owe you a drink.

That was something to look forward to. He replayed his last evening with Cole. The rimming had been pleasantly unanticipated. As had been the surprise blowjob that woke him up the next morning. Not wanting to be left out, he had flipped around and they'd engaged in a wonderful round of sixty-nine. He'd had to drag his ass out of there an hour later so he wouldn't be late for work.

His time with Cole had been unexpected. They'd clicked both socially and sexually. The ease he'd felt when he'd arrived at Cole's condo, the way he'd been handed a beer and then invited to watch the hockey game had been so natural he hadn't even questioned it. Cole, the man he'd always assumed to be buttoned-up and a bit reserved, had surprised him. Both by yelling and screaming at the hockey game, and by the unexpected swipe of his tongue across Owen's ass.

Yeah, that was awesome. They needed to do that again.

His cock strained in his pants. Awkward, given the toddler across the waiting room was now pointedly staring at him as she sucked her thumb. God, he hoped his dad would be done soon. His phone buzzed with another message from Cole.

I haven't been able to stop thinking about the other night.

Me either. I currently have a boner as I sit at the doctor's office.

Doctor? Everything okay?

The last thing he wanted to do was dump the shit with his dad on Cole. The other man had more than enough stuff to deal with right now without Owen adding to that pile.

All good. Just a normal checkup. He didn't like lying, but then again it was pretty much a white lie. It was a normal checkup for his dad, and hopefully everything was fine and he and his mom were overreacting to the situation. Hopefully.

Before Cole had a chance to respond, the nurse was standing at the door. "Mr. McGregor, can I see you for a second?"

Gotta go. Ttyl.

"Hey." He tucked his phone into his pocket.

The nurse looked over her shoulder. "I think Dr. Khan might be having a problem with your dad. Do you mind going in?"

Shit. "Of course."

The small exam room contained one chair and the table. His father was sitting in the middle of the table with his arms crossed and a scowl on his face.

"Dad?"

Dr. Khan was a petite woman with long black hair. She had it pulled into a low ponytail that rested across her shoulder. It made her look far younger than the midfifties he knew her to be. "Hi there, Mr. McGregor—"

His dad narrowed his gaze at them both. "That's *Owen*. I'm Mr. McGregor."

"Yes, I'm Owen. I hear the bear is causing you problems."

"He won't let me give him a physical, which is fine. But he also won't tell me any of the details of his problem. It makes my job a bit challenging."

"I don't have a problem. This one and my wife seem to think I do."

Owen had hoped his father would be cooperative, but apparently that was asking too much. "His personality has been changing. He's more argumentative, and Mom said that he's having a hard time with little things around the house. Nothing huge, but stuff that he'd never had issues with before. I think he's a bit confused as well. He's forgetting things that we'd agreed to ages ago."

Dr. Khan made some notes, throwing the occasional glance at his dad. Owen looked over and came up short when he realized his dad was crying. "What's wrong?"

This was wrong on so many levels, Owen couldn't get his head around it. His dad had always been strong, full of life. Sure he probably cried, but Owen had never seen him. Without waiting to be asked, he wrapped his arm around his dad and sat down on the exam table with him.

"Dad?"

"Ah, my boy." He shook his head. "I'm sorry."

"It's fine. We just want to help you."

"I know you do."

"Mr. McGregor, is there anything you can add to what your son said?"

His dad didn't look at the doctor, instead keeping his gaze fixed on his hands in his lap. "He's right. I'm forgetting stuff. But it's not little things. I'll go for a walk, and forget where I'm going. Then I won't recognize where I'm at. I ended up at the bar the other day, and I didn't remember anything about it."

That explained so many things. "How long?"

"I don't know. It was little things at first. I just assumed it was regular getting-old shit."

Dr. Khan came close and checked his blood pressure. "I want to send you for some blood work. Depending on what it shows, I may have to refer you to a neurologist. I'll ask Lynda to get that paperwork started."

His dad got up. "Washroom?"

"Down the hall, before the waiting room, on the left."

Owen waited for his dad to leave before he turned to face the doctor. He didn't want to ask, but given what he'd heard and what he knew, there was one question he needed to know the answer to. "Do you think it's Alzheimer's?"

Her frown told him more than he wanted to know. "That's a possibility. We'll also get a urine sample, and if he'll allow it today, I'll check his reflexes and ask about some other things. The neurologist would have to confirm Alzheimer's, but the tests will be able to tell us if there is something else going on."

"That seems unlikely."

"There are lots of things that could give a false positive. A cyst on his brain for example. There could be something damaged from his stroke that we weren't aware of or that's deteriorated. We'll find out. Don't assume the worst yet. I know it will be hard, but we won't have the results back until after the holidays. For the next few weeks, try and keep to his routine and make sure things are simple."

The drive back to his parents' house was quiet. He had tons of questions he wanted to ask, but his dad was in no mood to discuss anything. Before he got out of the car, Owen leaned over and put a hand on his dad's arm.

"I'm not going to force you to talk. I'm not going to tell you what to do. But I'm here for you and mom. Anything you need, anytime you need it, call me."

"I know."

"Dad?"

"Hmm."

"I love you. You know that, right?"

His dad looked at him, and for the first time all day, he smiled. He cupped the back of Owen's head, running his thumb through his hair. "You're a good boy. I love you too." And then he left.

The weight he'd felt when he'd first learned of his dad's stroke—the pressure on his shoulders and chest—came back. It was crap being an only child. He wanted nothing more than to reach out to someone, have them help carry part of this burden. But there was no one else, and he'd be damned if he'd let anything bad happen to his parents.

Cole slipped into the bar a few minutes before seven. He'd been distracted most of the day, ever since Owen had made the suggestion that they go out to bowl a bit tonight. Not that he was a bowler, but something about the idea of seeing Owen pitch balls down a lane appealed. Probably had something to do with being able to watch his ass.

The bar was busy given the time of night. Over half the tables were occupied and were covered with appetizers and mugs of beer. A good night for the bar meant a busy night for Owen. The seats around the bar were also full, but a few of the people didn't look as though they were staying long. Rather than taking up a table, Cole hovered around, waiting for an opportunity to swoop in and steal a spot.

Owen was currently chatting with a man who looked as though he'd walked straight out of a men's magazine. His suit was expensive looking, as was the cell phone in his hand. The man's gaze was locked onto Owen's, a laser-sharp intensity that anyone could see. Despite their one night of awesome sex, Cole really couldn't lay any claims to Owen's time or affections. But the sight of another man showing an interest in Owen didn't sit right with him.

Dear God, he might be jealous.

Eventually the man paid for his drinks and left the bar, but not before casting a glance back at Owen. Not wanting to take the chance that someone would steal the spot, Cole moved in quickly. If he happened to block the other dude's line of sight to Owen, well, that wasn't really his fault.

"Cole!" Owen grinned. The lines around his eyes looked more pronounced, and he had some dark circles forming. "I'm glad you made it."

"It's pretty busy in here tonight." As much as he wanted the opportunity to spend time with Owen, he didn't want to add more pressure. "Do you want to put this off?"

Owen opened his mouth to say something, but was immediately interrupted by a customer. Then a second and a third. Cole was many things, but selfish wasn't one. He waited until he caught Owen's eye and motioned that he was going to leave.

He got halfway to the door before Owen caught up with him. "Where are you going?"

"It's crazy in here, and it's only seven. You can't leave and go across town. Even for the wonderful sport of bowling."

"But I want to." Dear God, Owen was pouting again. It always seemed so out of character for this confident man, and yet it transformed Owen's face into something boyishly irresistible.

Shit, he really needed to resist.

"I'll take a rain check." There were always leftovers and holiday movies back at his place. "Give me a call once the bar is closed, and we can chat."

"No." There was something else going on with Owen, Cole could tell by the look on his face. "I have an idea. Follow me."

Owen led him through to the back of the bar, past the staff room where they'd had their breakfast. Owen said something to Jane before leading him to a staircase by a side door.

"My place is just up here. Jane is going to cover for me for a bit, and I'm going to fulfill my offer of bowling."

The stairs creaked as they went. He wouldn't admit it, but he was excited to see Owen's place. "How the hell are we going to bowl in your apartment?"

Owen looked down at him and grinned. "I have a Wii."

"Shit."

"Come on, it'll be fun. I have an unlimited supply of beer and everything."

Well, at least he wouldn't have to worry about gross bowling shoes.

He didn't know what to expect when he followed Owen through the door. Unlike his condo with its long, narrow entranceway, Owen's place was a completely open loft. Exposed beams lined the ceiling, giving the room an organic feel. Two walls were brick; one of those held three large windows. In the daytime, the place would be flooded with sunlight.

"Does this look out onto the street?"

Owen beelined to the fridge. "Yeah. I have to keep the blinds closed most of the time at night. I don't think people want to see my naked ass walking around here."

Somehow Cole doubted that. "It's a great space. I'm jealous."

"Dad ended up buying the building a decade ago after years of renting. I laid claim to here once the previous tenants finally moved out. It can be loud, but seeing as I work downstairs most nights, I don't have to worry about it." Owen handed him a beer and nodded toward the giant television on the wall. "Lots of room for my toys."

"We're watching the next Leafs game here." Maybe Wii bowling wouldn't be so bad after all. "Okay, let's do this before I change my mind."

It didn't take long for him to realize that Owen had a competitive streak. For every spare or strike Owen would land, there would be laughter and taunting. Thankfully, Cole had a younger sister who was exactly the same. He knew how to give as good as he got.

Making sure to line his next shot up perfectly, he had a chance to get a spare. Owen was tossing paper or something at him, trying to throw him off. "That's not going to work."

"Sure it will. Don't miss, Cole. Careful! Sure you want to put your foot there? I'd suggest shifting over a bit."

"I have a younger sister. There's nothing you can do to me that hasn't been done before." Focusing on his Wii character, he took one, two, three steps and released his virtual ball. "Yes!"

"No!" Owen collapsed against the pillow on his couch. "You bastard."

"And I believe I win this round." Cole's face ached, he'd been grinning so much. Downing the rest of his beer, he checked the time. "Do you need to get back?"

"Probably." Owen didn't move. "What are you up to for the rest of the night?"

"Not much. I have some chores to do around the condo. I'll probably check out some of the Christmas specials that are on. I have to admit that I've enjoyed my time off, even when I'm not slumming it with you."

"You don't have to leave." Owen looked surprised that he'd spoken. He pushed himself up and stared at Cole. "I mean, I won't have to work until close. Mike will shut down the kitchen soon and then come out and help behind the bar. I really only need to be there for another hour, hour and a half at most. If you want to hang out here and watch TV and wait, you're more than welcome to."

That was the most tempting offer he'd had in a long time. This didn't have to be about sex or a relationship. They were friends, who happened to have a great time together and wanted to keep hanging out. It was his school days all over again.

Plus, he really didn't want to be alone.

Owen's cell phone rang, interrupting before Cole could answer. Owen frowned as he checked the call display. "Sorry, one second. Hey." He moved away from Cole as he spoke.

Maybe it was the bar calling up, telling him that they needed him back. Owen lowered his voice as he spoke, but Cole couldn't help overhearing some of what he said.

"I know. I talked to him yesterday, and he seemed better. No. No. I just can't right now. Okay. I'll call you tomorrow. Bye."

"Everything all right?"

"Fine." It was clear from the look on Owen's face that everything was *not* fine. "Anyway, you're more than welcome to stay."

Seeing that look on Owen's face, he wanted to do something to help. He didn't even know what the issue was, but he hated knowing that Owen was hurting. It was the same way he'd always wanted to look after Steven, to make sure that he was okay.

God, was he really ready to start something like this again? Owen wasn't like Steven, not at all, and yet the old urges were there all the same—to shelter, to protect. Emotionally, he knew he wasn't in a place to be doing this. Owen was too much of a temptation in so many ways.

Maybe I should get some space...

He smiled, but it felt strained. "I think I'll head home to get some laundry done. We can get together again soon. Or we could always wait until after Christmas. Maybe skating or go see a movie?"

Owen's phone buzzed, and he looked down at a message. "I'm not a big fan of skating."

It was weird, but that was one thing Steven had never done, which Cole had loved. When they were talking, Steven never split his attention. In that moment, Cole had always been the most important thing in the world.

I miss that about Steven.

Damn it.

He cleared his throat. "Okay, well I'll let you go."

Owen leaned in as he came close, and placed a kiss on his cheek. "I'm sorry. I'll call you soon."

Walking down the stairs, his heart sank a tiny bit with each step he took. He was really just friends with Owen. They didn't owe one another anything. Things would work out. And he could learn to ignore that weight that settled on top of his heart until eventually it went away.

CHAPTER ELEVEN

Cole managed to get through the rest of his week without any problems. The day after his bowling event with Owen, he drove over to Steven's apartment and left his box of stuff with the superintendent. If nothing else, he wouldn't have to look at those reminders any longer.

By the time Saturday rolled around, he knew things were going to be okay. Christmas was only five days away now, which meant everywhere he went in Toronto, the city was decorated and looking beautiful. They had talked about going skating, and ever since then he hadn't been able to get it out of his mind. Cole wasn't going to call Owen to go with him, but the thought of being outside and getting some fresh air was appealing. He'd gotten his skates sharpened last night and was set to force himself out into the world today.

Hell, he might even be social.

The outdoor rink at Eglinton Park was packed with families and couples. It wasn't too cold for a December day, which meant lots of people had come out. The scent of street food made his stomach growl. He didn't normally go for that sort of thing, but why the hell not? It was Christmas, and he might as well treat himself. He'd grab a hot dog on his way home and hope he wouldn't regret the decision later with a bad case of indigestion.

It had been years since he'd done any skating. He'd played hockey as a kid and in a recreation league for a bit in his early twenties, but then work and life got in the way. His skates still fit, though they felt odd being on his feet after so long. The first few pushes sent a familiar ache through his ankles and feet as they adjusted to being up on the blades. Within a few minutes though, he was gracefully following the crowd in their lazy loop like he'd never stopped skating.

The activity gave him the opportunity to let his mind wander over the events of the last few weeks. Everything had been racing, from the fall through of the trip to Banff, to the breakup and then whatever the hell it had been with Owen. All that complication was easy to forget with the repetitive one-two push of his blades on ice.

After a few minutes, he got the strange feeling that he was being watched. There were lots of people at the rink and it shouldn't surprise him that he might catch someone's eye. But this didn't feel as though someone was taken with his looks or his slightly rusty skating technique. He looked around, trying to figure out who it might be.

Then someone came up beside him. He turned and was shocked to see Owen had fallen into step beside him.

"You." Not the most intelligent thing to say and more than a little obvious. "What are you doing here?"

"I was looking out my apartment window when I saw you leave with your skates. I grabbed mine and followed you here."

He should be upset that he'd been followed, that even after telling Owen he didn't want to see him until after Christmas he'd been stalked regardless. He should be, but he wasn't. "You know that's a bit creepy."

"Did I cross a line?" Owen's pout was back and cute as ever. "I can leave if you want."

He knew if he said the word, Owen would leave. There wouldn't be any hard feelings either. On his way home the other night, Cole's heart had grown heavy with the thought of not seeing Owen again. Now that he had him back, he didn't want to scare him away. But he hadn't lost his reservations, either.

"It's a public park. I have no say in who comes here to skate." He shoved his hands in his pockets, using his arms as a bit of a barrier. "I'm surprised to see you up this early. I assumed you worked until close most nights."

"I did. Didn't sleep well so I got up. Just a fluke that I happened to see you."

"A happy accident, then."

"Something like that."

They took a few more turns around the rink before he could figure out what to say next. "Christmas is in a few days. How long are you closing the bar for?"

"Christmas Eve, Christmas Day, and Boxing Day. Have you decided what you're going to do yet?"

"My sister and her husband are going to my parents'. I'll probably head over as well."

"Sounds fun." There was something odd in Owen's voice. "I'll spend the morning with my folks as well."

It wasn't any of Cole's business to interfere with whatever was happening in Owen's life. But the bartender looked as though he needed a distraction of his own. Considering what he'd done for Cole, the least Cole could do was offer a light distraction in return. He took Owen by the arm and tugged him over to the side of the rink.

"Where are we going?"

"I'm hungry, and my feet are sore. It's been a long time since I've done this. I was thinking about grabbing a hot dog and a coffee. It would be nice to have some company."

Cole sat down and worked on removing his skates. His feet ached, and when he finally got his boots back on, he had that phantom-blade-in-the-middle-of-his-foot sensation. Owen was still standing there, looking down at him with a weird expression.

"What?" Cole shook his head. "I'm heading out either way. If you want to stay and skate, go for it."

Owen glanced around before he sat beside him on the bench and removed his own skates. "I got the impression the other night that you didn't want anything more to do with me."

There was that. "Not really."

"I came after you to apologize for whatever I'd done. I've replayed everything over in my head, but I can't figure out where I'd screwed up."

That was the problem, Owen *hadn't* done something wrong. Cole was paranoid at best. There was nothing wrong with being cautious, about keeping his distance from a man he could easily lose himself in. But that didn't mean he should sacrifice the beginnings of what was turning out to be a good friendship.

"Honestly, you were fine. The last few weeks have been overwhelming. I keep forgetting that Steven left me only earlier this month. I'm overreacting to everything. Right now I need a friend and you've been a better one to me than I've been to you." He got to his feet, holding his skates by the blades. "I'm sorry. If you'd like, I'll buy you some lunch to make it up to you."

One moment Owen looked as though he might cry, and the next he was grinning like a fool. "That sounds awesome. If you're up for it, I found out that *Silent Night, Deadly Night* is playing on-demand."

"A Christmas horror movie?"

"Apparently a really bad one."

That was normally the last type of movie Cole would want to watch. But saying yes meant spending time with Owen, something that he now wanted to do more than anything. "Why not. If it sucks though, I'm out of there."

"Fair enough. I promise it will be horri-bad in all respects, but hilariously fun. At least that's what I've been told."

"You haven't seen it?"

Owen shook his head, grinning even more broadly. "I'm always up for something new to try."

They fell into step on their way to the street vendor. Two hot dogs and fries in hand, they chatted as they walked and ate. Cole knew in his heart that a relationship with Owen was foolish, especially after his realization of how little he knew the other man. Typical him, moving from acquaintance to friendship to relationship in his head in the span of days. This was why his relationships didn't work out. Unrealistic expectations.

Unrealistic expectations. But forewarned was forearmed, right? All Cole needed to do was keep his brain from making that leap to relationship mode and everything would be good.

This time when he made the trip up the stairs to Owen's apartment, he was in a far better mind-set. Owen got them two beers each, and they took up residence on his couch to watch . . . well, whatever the hell this movie was supposed to be.

It didn't take long for the two of them to start groaning and heckling the action on the screen. The movie was a typical eighties horror film, complete with big-busted girls and an evil nun at an orphanage. Still, there were some good jumps that had him squirming in his seat. He really didn't like horror movies.

Owen took another sip of his beer and stretched his arm out along the back of the couch. "This thing got banned at the time. Too controversial having Santa with an ax. Apparently it only played for two weeks in the theaters."

"I can appreciate that. If I had kids, I wouldn't want them to see this and freak." Without thinking, Cole let his head fall back against Owen's arm.

The contact drew his attention away from the movie and refocused it on Owen. He had on a long-sleeved cotton shirt. The material was soft against the back of Cole's neck, and he gently moved so he could enjoy the sensation of it against his skin. Once he'd stopped moving, Owen shifted again; this time his fingers brushed against Cole's hairline.

A shiver raced through Cole, and his cock hardened. Shit, this wasn't right. He couldn't lead Owen on again, taking something when he knew there wasn't a future for them. He needed to stop this. Now.

"Owen—"

He sucked in a surprised breath when Owen cupped the back of his head, leaned in, and nipped on his earlobe. "I haven't been able to get you out of my head."

Fuck. "Owen, I'm not sure we should do this."

"I'll stop if you want." He nuzzled his nose against the side of Cole's neck, kissing and licking a trail across his skin. "If you really want me to. Just say the word."

This was such a bad idea. A terrible mistake. "Don't stop."

Owen sighed and continued his exploration of Cole's neck. They began to make out as the movie played in the background. There was no urgency to what they were doing, no expectation that anything else needed to happen. The brush of lips and tongues, gentle nips and soft moans allowed Cole to relax and simply enjoy.

It was fucking awesome.

Owen kept his hands mostly above Cole's belt, rubbing and squeezing his arms and chest. It was nice to know that he was respecting Cole's previous reluctance, but the more they kissed, the more Cole needed things to move to the next step.

He took Owen's hand and slid it down to the hard bulge in his pants. "Look what you do to me."

"I want you too." Owen shifted so Cole could feel Owen's hard cock against his leg. "I'm going to suck you."

Thank God.

"Then I'm going to get some lube and a condom and fuck you over my couch."

Jesus save me. "Hurry."

Cole had never undressed that quickly before. He popped a button getting his shirt off, and for once didn't care about the state of his clothing. Owen seemed to be just as frantic, pulling and tossing clothing without looking. Once he was naked, Cole picked up the remote and turned the television off. "Don't want that shit on anymore."

"Yeah, not the sort of thing you want to fuck to." Owen pulled him hard against his chest and bit his chin. "You drive me fucking insane. I want to do all these things to you. Just you."

"Like what?"

"I want to fuck you hard and fast. I want to spank you so I know what noises you make. I want you to fuck me on my back, your hands on my throat so I feel possessed by you." The intensity of his gaze matched that of his words. "I've never been like this with another person before. This is crazy. I want to do everything with you. Everything."

The thought equally terrified and thrilled Cole. This wasn't a friendship or even a causal sex thing. Owen was on a path that he didn't know if he could follow. The smart thing would be to stop things right then, get dressed, and walk away before they both got hurt.

He was beginning to realize that he wasn't a smart man. "Get the lube and condom." He swallowed hard. "I need you to fuck me now. Right the hell now."

That was it. Owen left him to get what they needed, and Cole moved behind the couch. He leaned over the back of it, spread his legs, and waited. He knew the second Owen returned because the other man groaned.

"That's a sight I would never get tired of seeing."

Cole reached behind and smacked his ass. "Don't spend too much time gawking."

"No worries about that."

Owen came up behind him and squeezed his ass cheeks with both hands. He kneaded and pulled at his ass, until Cole's body shook. He tried to push against Owen, hoping the other man would take the hint, but clearly he had a different plan.

The first smack of Owen's hand across his ass surprised the hell out of him. The sting from the contact burned for a moment before dissolving into an almost pleasant heat. Owen continued kneading his skin. "Like that?"

Did he? Spanking hadn't even been something he'd thought of before now. "Not sure."

Owen spanked his other ass cheek, though not quite as hard as he had the first time. Cole's cock swayed from the impact, bringing the head into contact with the couch. His body was revved up, ready for anything that Owen threw at him.

"Your body should be illegal." Owen placed a series of kisses down Cole's spine to his tailbone. "I've never been this hard for a guy before. Ever."

The lube-slick finger slipped easily into his ass, and the subsequent sensation skittered through his body. Owen worked his body open quickly, and Cole felt Owen's hands shaking as he moved around him. The crinkle of a condom wrapper cued him to widen his stance, getting ready for the fucking he wanted more than anything at that moment.

One hand, then the other on his hips, and finally the long, slow side of Owen's cock into his waiting body. Cole shuddered as he leaned his forehead against the top of the couch cushion. Owen moved in and out of him at a painfully slow rate. Every inch of his cock filled Cole, stretched him wide until he couldn't breathe. The uncomfortable burn quickly eased away as his muscles relaxed, and Owen was finally free to take him however he wanted.

"Fuck me, Owen."

"As you wish."

Cole cried out at the abrupt change of pace, his cock instantly leaking at the pounding his prostate was taking. He didn't want this to end—the intensity, the pleasure, the way Owen seemed to know exactly what he needed even before he did.

Case in point, he was half a second away from grabbing his cock when Owen beat him to it. He started stroking Cole's shaft in time with his thrusts. Pleasure zipped through Cole, spreading to fill every inch of his body. It wasn't going to take long to push him over the edge, but he didn't care. This wasn't like their first time together. The intimacy had been almost too much, too soon. The raw nature of their fucking now, yes, this was better. He understood this, wanted it. Had never shared anything even remotely close to this with anyone.

This was all Owen.

Owen leaned forward and bit down on Cole's shoulder. "Come."

Fuck. Cole squeezed his eyes shut, thrust into Owen's magic hand, and came hard. His muscles tensed, and his hips bucked into Owen's touch. He couldn't think beyond *Yes, more.* Finally, after what could have been an eternity, the pleasure receded enough that he was able to come back to his senses. Owen had released Cole's cock and how gripped both of his hips. He could feel his cum on his skin where Owen touched him. It was wonderfully messy. Owen was still holding on, but Cole sensed he wasn't going to last much longer.

The stuttering rhythm picked up speed once again. Cole braced himself, thrusting back to meet Owen. His legs shook from the strain of Owen against him, but he didn't care. He didn't want to stop, not until Owen came.

"Fuck me, Owen. Come on."

Fingers dug into his hips, and finally Owen slammed into him hard and cried out. It was a primal roar of pleasure as cum filled the condom. Cole was the one who felt owned, possessed by Owen. He was safe and sated, at the mercy of the man behind him.

And damn it if he didn't like it.

Owen pulled out and placed several kisses across his back. "Holy shit."

Cole laughed as he pushed himself up, questioning if his legs would be able to hold him after all that. "I agree."

He didn't get far, as Owen wrapped him into a hug. As frantic as their fucking had been, their shared embrace was a place of calm.

Their breathing synced up as he ran his hands through Owen's hair. "That was . . . awesome."

"And unexpected." Owen kissed him soft and slow. "After you left the other day, I didn't think I'd be in this position again."

Cole closed his eyes, not wanting his brain to kick in and ruin the moment. "Yeah. Me either to be honest."

This wasn't the time or place for him to start thinking about the future. Christmas was in a few days, and he wanted nothing more than to spend time with his family, eat, drink, and maybe have some fun with Owen.

Nothing else. No relationship business. No Steven or what his leaving meant.

Nothing.

"Want to take a shower?" Owen's question jerked him back to reality.

"No. I wouldn't say no to a cloth though. You messed me up." The cum on his hip had already dried and was flaking off.

"I'd apologize, but I won't lie to you this close to Christmas." Owen grinned. "Let me get you something."

They chatted as they cleaned up and got dressed. Then they moved to the couch for some postcoital cuddling. Their conversation drifted from random topics to spaces of quiet. It was nice. Peaceful. It was also the first time he'd shared something like this with another man.

"Hey." Cole pushed away from Owen, but took his hand. "I know I've said this before, but thank you. I'm not sure I would have been okay with Steven leaving me the way he did if it wasn't for you."

"You're welcome."

As simple as that, Cole's heart melted another degree. How could he resist Owen and his loving, easygoing nature? Why would he even want to?

Because you don't know him, not really.

But that didn't mean that he couldn't take the time to fix that little problem. It was simple enough to do.

He cleared his throat. "I was wondering if you might want to go out on a date. With me. Not something designed to make me forget Steven, but something that will let me get to know you. I think I could find myself falling in love with you very quickly, and I don't want to repeat past mistakes. I want to go into things with my eyes open."

He wasn't looking at Owen as he spoke, nerves and embarrassment prevented that. But when Owen lifted his chin and kissed him hard, Cole knew he didn't have anything to worry about.

"You idiot. Of course."

He huffed out the breath he'd been holding. "Good. Great."

"We can work out the details later." Owen pulled Cole back against him and grabbed the remote. "First, I want to see the end of the movie."

"You're kidding. It's awful."

"Shh. I like the way you lean against me in the scary parts. Like I can protect you from Santa."

Cole settled into his spot against Owen's side and relaxed. Maybe this rebound thing with Owen wouldn't be like all the rest. For once, things seemed to be going his way.

CHAPTER TWELVE

Owen fiddled with his tie in the mirror for what felt like the tenth time in two minutes. He hadn't worn one since he'd quit working for Black Shield and hadn't missed the noose even once. But he'd agreed to go out to a nice restaurant with Cole to celebrate a holiday meal before they were both pulled apart with previously arranged Christmas celebrations. That meant a dress shirt, tie, and jacket.

Thankfully, he made it look good.

"Whoa, boss." Moe skidded to a stop and stared at him. "You're going to break some hearts."

"Thanks." He really was, wasn't he?

"I just wanted to let you know that Jane is running late, but Brad is going to stay later to cover until she arrives."

All thoughts of his date flew from his mind. "Do you need me to stay? Brad has been here since noon."

"No." Moe held up his hands and backed away. "No way. Jane was very specific that you were under no circumstance to stay. I assume she knows all about your . . . whatever it is you're doing tonight. She won't be long."

Jane was his right-hand woman when it came to the bar. She was also a great friend who'd always been there for him. She had taken one look at his face after Cole had left and knew something good had happened between them. Hell, she'd been the one to suggest the restaurant and book reservations for them. If he did anything to ruin tonight, she'd most likely kick his ass.

Still, the bar came first. "Fine. But if she doesn't show up by ten, I expect a call. I'm taking my date out for supper, and we should be done by then."

"Deal." Moe smiled. "It's nice to see you happy. Have a good time tonight, boss."

"Thanks. I will."

Well, he would as long as he wasn't late. Cole had agreed to drive them and was probably already waiting for him to get his ass in gear. His phone chose that moment to buzz.

I'm out front.

No more time to primp. He grabbed his overcoat and left through the side door. Cole was sitting in his Lexus in front of McGregor's. Owen's heart pounded a bit faster at the sight of him behind the glass. He'd never had this strong of a reaction to anyone, man or woman, before. There was just something about Cole, a calmness that he craved. If things went the way he hoped, then maybe, just maybe he'd convince Cole to take things from casual to something more.

Heat from the car blasted his face as he got into the passenger seat. "Hey."

The smell of cologne and shampoo washed over him half a second before Cole leaned in and kissed him. "Hey yourself. You look fantastic."

Owen felt himself blush. "Thanks. You too." He didn't care if it was overstepping, he snuck another quick kiss.

Cole grinned. "Let's head out before we're late. Traffic is crap tonight."

They fell into an easy back-and-forth conversation about nothing in particular. It was the same type of banter his parents had engaged in over the years. Not recently though.

"I've heard this place is really good." Cole pulled into the public parking. "We'll have to walk, but it's only about half a block."

"I'm all set."

The night air was crisp, making it necessary to keep coats buttoned and gloves on. Owen noticed that Cole didn't have any on, and knew he'd be cold even if it was a short walk. He pulled his left-hand glove off and offered it to him.

Cole frowned. "What's this for?"

"Your hand."

"But you need your glove."

Owen held up his right hand. "I have one."

Cole shook his head. "And how are you going to keep your other hand warm?"

"I was hoping you'd ask that." Owen took Cole's bare hand and laced their fingers together. "There."

Cole looked at where their hands met, and chuckled. "You're crazy."

"Probably. Let's go before they give our table away. I'm starving."

The restaurant was a small intimate place. The long narrow dining area was packed with tables, each one filled with people. A bubbly older woman greeted them at the door, menus in hand. "Welcome to Horizon."

"Hi." Owen stepped forward. "Reservation for two under McGregor."

"Yes, come with me, please."

They weaved their way through the throng of people and tables until they were led to the back. It wasn't ideal, they were surrounded on all sides by others, but Owen figured it was better than nothing.

Being who he was, Owen picked up the drink menu first. "Wow, bit overpriced."

"I wouldn't have a clue. I always expect to pay more when I'm eating out, so I never think about it."

"The downside to owning a bar: you know what the markup is. Or should be in this case."

He found a decent wine that wasn't crazy expensive and ordered a bottle.

Cole grinned. "Are you trying to get me drunk? I have to drive home, remember."

"I'm sure you can handle a glass or two of wine. Besides, we can always cab it and come back for the car tomorrow."

"I've never left my vehicle behind as much as I have when I'm around you. If we go out again, we should just take a cab."

Wine came and was quickly followed by appetizers and entrées. He didn't want to stare, but the longer they were together, the more he couldn't look away from Cole. His blue eyes sparkled and his black hair fell across his forehead, tempting Owen to reach across and push it aside. Damn it, he was becoming obsessed with Cole. Which might or might not be a good thing.

Cole leaned back against his chair, his glass of wine in his hand. "So you're going to your parents' place for Christmas Eve?"

"Yeah. Mom has already got my holiday planned out." She needed help with a few repairs around the house. Some things that his dad would normally take care of, but that she didn't want to ask him to do until they got the test results back.

Cole frowned. "What's that?"

"What's what?"

"You said one thing, but something else crossed your mind. Your whole expression changed. What's wrong?"

He'd promised himself he wouldn't dump his family stress on Cole. The other man was just starting to come out from the cloud that had been on him since his dumbass ex dumped him. Owen could handle his parents, the bar, and everything else. Even if it would be good to talk to someone else about things. He wouldn't do that to Cole. Not yet.

"Ah, you know what it's like. Family at the holidays." He swallowed down a large gulp of wine.

Cole didn't look as though he were buying it, but he didn't push either. "My sister loves to torture me about my love life whenever the family gets together."

"Will she be sad that you're single?"

"Hell no. She hated Steven from the moment I told her about him. I guess she saw something in him that I didn't."

"Told her? You mean she hadn't met him?"

"No. I don't know why, but it never quite worked out, him meeting my family. I guess it doesn't matter now. Angie won't be happy about how we broke up, but I know she'll say that I'm better off without him."

"I like your sister. Personally, I can't wait to meet her."

Cole put his glass down and sat a bit straighter. "Nice of you to say, but you don't know her."

Okay . . .

"And I don't know much about your family either. You took over the bar from your dad, right? He had a stroke?"

"I did, and he did." He really didn't want to talk about his dad. Not when they were having such a great night.

"What is he doing now that he's retired? Is the stroke still affecting him or is he better? Is he another bowler?"

"I'm not really—"

"My parents love to travel. They're out of the country almost as much as they're in it. No Florida for them yet, but they do tend to hang out on cruise ships. Your parents do anything like that?"

"Cole—"

"It's just I don't really know much about your family. You run a bar and used to work at a computer company—"

"Internet security."

"Family is important to me. So I'm curious."

The way Cole said those words made Owen feel there was more to this conversation than he realized. "Family is important to me as well. I gave up my career for my family so we could keep the bar. I wouldn't do that if I didn't feel that they mattered."

"That's good. These are the sorts of things I want to know."

Something was going on with Cole. He wasn't angry; if anything he seemed anxious, or excited. Maybe a mix of the two. Owen reached out and took his hand. "Are you okay?"

"I've been thinking a lot about Steven today, about our relationship. One of the things that I hadn't thought about was how little I knew about him outside of what we shared. I'd spoken to his mother on the phone, but in the six months we'd been together, I'd never actually met her."

"You want to meet my parents?" That was the last thing he wanted to do to Cole. Not with everything as uncertain as it was. With his dad's behavior unpredictable at best, he'd worry that something would be said to upset or offend Cole. "We're not even dating."

Cole opened his mouth to speak, but nothing came out.

Owen groaned. "I didn't mean that I would never want you to meet them. If we were, you know, a couple or something, then yeah. But we're not. Are we?" God, he was a fucking idiot. He couldn't screw this conversation up any more if he'd tried. "Cole?"

"No. We're not. You're right. I'm not over Steven yet. I can't think about another relationship." He drank the rest of his wine and picked up the dessert menu. "They have traditional plum pudding as a special. I think I might order some."

Owen sat and stared at him, not knowing exactly what had happened. Tonight was supposed to be an opportunity for them to get to know one another, but it was also a chance for Owen to forget his troubles for a bit. Talking about his dad, about how stressed out his mom was, wasn't something he wanted to do. Surely Cole would understand that?

Right?

He could clear everything up a little—*Actually dad is sick and I'd rather not talk about it*—but the words wouldn't come. Cole wasn't the type of person to simply let things rest. He'd want to repay Owen for helping him with his Steven problem, would want to help. The last thing Owen wanted was to involve him in that. He wanted to keep Cole to himself. So he said nothing and hoped things would settle.

It wasn't until Cole dropped him off at the bar that he realized he'd made the wrong decision. He leaned over to kiss Cole, but instead of the warmth of his lips, he was met with a soft cheek.

"I'm glad we did this." Cole spoke without looking at him. "I . . . Thanks for everything."

He knew he should simply say good-night and get out of the car. He should leave everything alone. Cole was still hurting from his breakup, no matter how fine he'd seemed the other day. It was childish for Owen to be hurt by the rejection, and yet, he was human.

"I know you're upset with me. I've tried to be there for you. Maybe I've tried a bit too hard. I'll leave you be for now. When you're ready, if you're ready, you have my number. You know where I live. Hell, just come to the bar for a drink. I'll be there. Good night."

The temperature had dropped from when they'd left, making his breath visible as he huffed. He headed straight for the bar, not wanting to be alone. He needed the noise, the company of strangers to help push this feeling of dread from him. Cole would figure things out on his own. Owen had the bar and his family to sort through.

Only time would tell if they'd have room for each other in their lives.

CHAPTER THIRTEEN

The last place in the world Cole wanted to be the evening of December twenty-third was the Eaton Centre. The crowds were thick with people desperately searching for *one final thing*. Cole couldn't claim to be in any better shape. He still needed to find a gift for his mother and *one final thing* for Angie. He'd originally intended to bring her back something from Banff, which wasn't in the cards now. So here he was, caught in a throng as he searched for something that didn't scream *last-minute gift*.

A group of laughing teenage girls bumped into him, only to turn around and giggle once they got past. God, he had to find something for his mom fast so he could get the hell out of there. Each time he approached a store he made a judgment call about the length of the checkout line versus the chances he'd find something she'd like within. The kitchen gadget store was always a good idea, and it didn't look too insane at the moment.

He sidestepped several shoppers and made his way toward the glassware section. His mom loved her wine. He could get her one of those fancy glasses with a cute saying painted on. A nice bottle of red wine to go with it. He picked one up that announced *Winos Have Class* and smiled. Yeah, she'd like that. Maybe a big box of chocolates too—

"Cole?"

He'd heard the expression "time standing still," but had never experienced it before then. He turned to see Steven at the opposite end of the aisle, staring at him. It was strange—for a moment Cole wasn't even certain that it *was* Steven. He wasn't supposed to be here. He was supposed to be off somewhere with the love of his life, his *fiancé*.

Instead he was standing in the glassware section of a department store and staring at Cole.

"What are you doing here?" His voice cracked as the words forced their way past the lump in his throat. "I thought you'd left." *Left me behind.*

Steven put down the box he'd been holding and made his way closer. He stopped half a step away, but far too close for Cole's liking. The younger man looked off. "Yeah. Then we came back."

"What's wrong?" He didn't need to be told there was a problem. Steven wore his emotions on his face.

"Adam . . ." Steven shook his head. "I'd forgotten a few things about him. Some of which I didn't miss when we broke up. Bad habits." Steven reached out and ran a finger down the back of Cole's hand. "How are you?"

Just peachy. You broke my heart two weeks before Christmas only to show up again when I'm doubting my maybe-relationship with my bartender. Fantastic! "I'm living."

"Cole, I'm so sorry. You know I never intended to hurt you that way. Adam didn't either. He didn't know I'd moved on."

"Had you though? Moved on?" It wasn't something he'd really thought that much about before then. "Adam had always been on your mind when we were together. Hadn't he?"

Steven's lips tightened into a line before he nodded. "I guess that's true."

"Where is he?"

"We went to Montreal after . . . the airport. I was able to get my ticket changed." Steven shook his head. "Typical Adam. We went for five days and then had to come back. He'd forgotten about a meeting he had for his job, so here we are. It's fine though, it's given me time to think."

No.

A sense of dread filled Cole and pooled in his stomach. He didn't want Steven to continue, to say the words he knew were coming.

Steven swayed closer. "The irony is now that I have him back in my life, all I've been able to think about is you."

Fuck.

"When I saw Adam at the airport, he was all I could register. When he smiled at me, when he proposed, that was all I could see. I'd forgotten about the way he'd get so focused on work that he'd forget to talk to me for hours on end. I'd blocked the way he'd flirt with other men right in front of me, even if it was something he didn't intend."

Steven reached out and took his hand. "When I got home the other day, my super had the box of my things you'd left for me. Seeing it brought a lot of things back. I'd forgotten how loved you made me feel. How you'd focus on me when I was talking, the way you listened. I miss that. I miss you."

And there it was. The other shoe finally dropped.

Cole had fought his way through two weeks of heartache, insecure about his ability to have a serious relationship, all because Steven had impulsively left him for his old flame. It would have been horrible if Owen hadn't been there to help him through the worst of it.

Owen . . .

No, he had to focus on Steven, had to see this through to the end. It was the only way he'd be able to move on.

He squeezed Steven's hand. "Let's not do this here. There's a Starbucks in the food court. We can sit and talk."

Steven brightened and smiled. "Awesome."

They didn't speak as they made their way through the crowds. Steven went in search of a table while Cole bought and paid for their drinks. It was the natural pattern of their relationship, one they didn't even need to address. The time apart gave him the opportunity to catch his breath and think. Steven was engaged to another man, and Cole had no claims over him. He wasn't even certain he wanted that any longer. Still, he owed it to both of them to have this conversation.

It took him a minute to find Steven in the sea of weary holiday shoppers. Weaving his way once again through the throng of people, he set Steven's drink in front of him. "Here you go."

"Thanks."

They both sipped their drinks, sneaking glances at one another. He knew he'd have to be the one to start this, he was always the one who kick-started their conversations. He took a breath and cupped his coffee in his hands. "So, you're engaged."

"I am." Steven blushed. "That sounds so weird."

"It's quite the Christmas present." Cole looked at him, really looked hard. Steven was young and full of life, but lacked confidence. "You're questioning your decision?"

Steven nodded once. "I'm twenty-five. I feel like I'm still figuring shit out. When I saw Adam at the airport and then he got down on one knee, all I could think of was: this is it, my dream come true. Then on the drive back to my place I kept hearing your voice in the back of my head saying, 'Are you sure you want this?'"

At least he wasn't yelling and crying in Steven's memory. "*Do* you want this? I know Adam hurt you when he left you for the job, and I understand why you were happy when he came back. But this has to be right for you."

Steven slid his hand across the table and pressed his knuckles to Cole's. "You and Adam are so different. You're thoughtful where he's impulsive. He and I are so much alike, I keep wondering if I should have stayed with you. I need your balance to keep me grounded."

Cole froze. What he saw was a man who didn't know what he wanted from life. Someone who wanted someone else to be in charge of the hard decisions he was faced with. He didn't want a partner; Steven wanted a manager. Two weeks ago, Cole would have been okay with that position, but not any longer.

"Steve, I care about you. I probably always will."

Steven pulled back. "But?"

"But the last two weeks have put some things into perspective for me." God, how to word this without sounding like an asshole? "When we first got together, I knew you were hurting. I wanted to make things better. I wanted to be the man to save you. That says more about me than you. I had this need to be a savior, because in my experience that was the way people saw me. You going back to Adam was a wake-up call for me. Being that man wasn't who I wanted to be anymore. I didn't want to be the rebound guy. I wanted to be the first choice."

Owen had wanted him. Owen had been concerned for him, had been the one to put his needs ahead of Owen's. It was the first relationship he had been a part of where that had been the case. Regardless of how little time they'd been together—how neither of them had been willing to call what they'd been doing a *relationship*— what he'd shared with Owen had been different, wonderful. While there were no guarantees that if they got into a relationship things would work out any better, at least they were starting in a place of mutual respect and want.

First, he needed to make sure Steven was okay. "I know you never meant to hurt me. I'm not mad at you for going back to Adam. But it all happened quickly. You need to take time to make sure he's the right one for you. That you're making this decision because it's what you want, not what you think you need. Since I've met you, you've let others take control, Steve. This is on you now. To stay or go."

"Go back to you?" The hope in his eyes was heartbreaking.

"No. You leaving me opened my eyes. I'll always be there for you, but only as your friend. I can't give you more than that. We're not good for one another. Not really."

Steven sat back and looked away. "So what do I do?"

"Take some time. Think about what you want from your life. You're engaged, but that's not the end of the world. Don't get married for a year. Or two. You talked about wanting to go back to school. Go do that. If Adam loves you, then he'll support you. You need to figure out where the pieces of your life go, otherwise you'll never be happy, no matter who you're with."

He'd never been one to take his own advice, but this time Cole knew he was right. He wanted a partner, not just a lover. He wanted someone who enjoyed hockey, who was willing to try new things, but not afraid of routine. He wanted a best friend he couldn't keep his hands off. Of all the men he'd been with over the years, Owen had been the first person to fit into all those roles.

Cole had been blinded by his broken heart, blinded to the gem of a soul who'd reached out to him in his time of need. He wanted Owen.

If Owen was willing to have him.

Steven cleared his throat, drawing his attention. "You look like you've come to a decision yourself."

"Yeah, I think I might have." The dread that had built up in his stomach dissipated, washed away with the last gulp of his coffee. "I just hope things aren't too late to make them right."

"Well, you told me that if things were meant to be, then they would work out. I have a feeling the universe owes you this one." Steven got to his feet and placed a kiss to Cole's cheek. "Take care. And if you're okay with it, I'm going to keep your number. Just in case I need some advice."

"Sure. Merry Christmas, Steve."

He watched Steven disappear into the crowd and knew that things were over between them. He hadn't realized how much he'd needed that closure. To know that despite the way they'd broken up, it was in fact the right thing. The weight of uncertainty had lifted, and he was able to move on.

He knew in his heart that what he'd shared briefly with Owen was better than all the months he'd had with Steven wrapped together. Sure, Owen had held things back from him. They weren't officially dating and had only had a fling for two weeks. He was an idiot to think that there wouldn't be things Owen would want to keep to himself. That didn't mean Cole didn't want to know, to learn what they were.

Time was working both for and against them. He wanted more of it with Owen, but he was terrified he'd screwed things up. It was also a day and a half before Christmas, not the best time of year to be laying his heart on the line. Still, it was better to be up-front, give Owen time to think, and find out if he wanted to take the chance and see where things could go between them.

Jumping to his feet, he knew what he had to do. The bar was going to be open until 2 a.m. and then Owen would be gone to spend the day before Christmas with his parents. Cole would grab a gift for his mom and then he'd go see Owen.

Maybe, just maybe, he'd get his holiday wish in the form of a sexy bartender.

CHAPTER FOURTEEN

The bar was packed, which meant Owen had all hands on deck. He, Jane, and Moe were behind the bar, getting drinks to the servers and patrons as quickly as they could. His cheeks ached from the perma-grin he'd worn for hours. As he shoved a full tray of cranberry vodka twists to the edge of the bar for pickup, he glanced at the clock. Twelve forty. He'd been working since open, and he was more than ready for closing time.

Jane bumped into him, a weary smile on her face. "This is busier than last year."

"I guess all our promotions are actually working." A little too well given the state of his staff. "I'll have to hire more help next year."

"Can't hurt. It will give us more opportunities to switch off. Plus you look like shit."

A customer asked for a pitcher of draft, pulling Jane away.

The last thing he wanted to do was get into a conversation about how he was feeling. She didn't know that it had nothing to do with the bar, working crazy hours, or even his dad. Since Cole had walked out on him, he had felt like he looked. It was weird how much he missed the other man. If he hadn't been so worried about protecting Cole, he would have talked about his problems with him.

He cleared his throat. "Last call, everyone!"

A collective groan went up through the crowd before a flurry of final drink orders came rushing in. Thirty minutes later, the crowd started to dissipate and they were able to breathe. He didn't want them to be around too late, knowing his team had more than earned their tips and time off after the past week. They'd get through their cleanup and he'd send them all home at a reasonable hour. Then they'd have to get ready for New Year's Eve and the insanity that would ensue.

It didn't take too long for them to usher everyone out the door. There were a few stragglers, but Moe was on bouncer duty tonight. His punishment for avoiding puker duty two weeks ago. That freed Owen to take a quick inventory and sort out the cash. He had just enough energy left to close things, and then he planned to collapse in his bed and sleep.

"Boss?"

Owen managed not to groan. "Yes, Moe?"

"We have a . . . straggler. He won't leave the booth."

God, if someone could cut me some slack, it would be awesome. "You're a bouncer, Moe. Go bounce."

"Trust me, I've tried. I think you'll have to deal with this one." He at least had the decency to look embarrassed. "Sorry."

"Fine. Where is he?"

"Back booth. Near the bathrooms."

Owen shoved the inventory sheets at Moe. "Finish this please." And he was off to kick the merrymaker out of his bar.

This was the last thing he needed, but it came with the territory. "Hey, buddy, the bar is closing up. Time to head out."

"I was hoping I could speak to the owner."

He stopped dead at the sound of Cole's voice. He was sitting in the booth, a nearly full glass of beer in his hand.

"What are you doing here?" Okay, that came out harsher than he'd intended. "I mean, I thought you were with your family."

"I will be but not until Christmas morning." He swallowed down part of his beer. "I know you're busy, but I was hoping we could talk."

Something about Cole was different from the last time Owen had seen him. First off, he was smiling. Always a good sign. Owen looked over his shoulder to where Jane, Moe, and several other staff weren't bothering to hide the fact they were watching him. Jane even shot him a wink, which was all the encouragement he needed to slide into the booth opposite Cole.

Not entirely sure where this conversation was going, he grabbed Cole's beer and took a swig. "You look good."

"You're exhausted. It was crazy in here tonight."

This was it, his chance to set things right. Since Cole had walked away, Owen had regretted not sharing his problems with him. There weren't any excuses now.

"I am tired. It's not just the bar though." The dam burst and all the words he'd been holding back spilled forth. "My dad's sick. Not just from the stroke. His behavior has become erratic over the past six months or so. My mom didn't tell me until last week because she was scared that I'd taken on too much with the bar. But he'd shown up here angry and confused, so she couldn't hide it any longer. I haven't known you long, not really. And the last thing I wanted to do was dump my problems on you when you were still working everything out with your ex. I should have been up-front about all this when you asked and for that I'm sorry. I'm still not great about asking for help."

When he looked up from the spot on the table that he'd been staring at, he was surprised to see Cole frowning. Shit, maybe he'd made a mistake after all.

Cole reached out and took his hand. "I'm sorry you're going through that. I understand why you wouldn't want to share everything. I was so wrapped up in myself that I'm ashamed I didn't see your reactions for what they really were. It also confirms what I already suspected about you."

Owen's heart pounded a bit faster. "What's that?"

"That you're a good man with good intentions. You're the type of person who helps strangers, will take the shirt off his back for a friend, and lay his life on the line for his family. I'm honored to be your friend."

Friend. It felt as though what they shared was so much more than friendship. "I know it's only been two weeks. I know there are things I still want to know about you, your family. I'm sure there's lots you want to know about me."

Cole smiled, and Owen's heart did a somersault. "Yeah, there's lots of stuff for us to share, but I think I already know the important part."

"What's that?"

Cole laced their fingers together. Instead of answering his question, Cole threw him for a loop. "I ran into Steven today."

"What?" He somehow held himself still. "I thought he was away?"

"They came back early. He was Christmas shopping."

"What happened?"

"We talked. He's not sure he did the right thing. He wanted me to tell him he did. Or to take him back."

He hadn't considered that Cole might want to go back to Steven. Not after everything he'd been through to this point. "Did you?"

"Of course not. How could I when I'm in love with you?"

Joy exploded inside him. He had to swallow twice to get his voice to work. "What?"

"I think, quite possibly, that I might be a teeny bit in love with you." Cole leaned down and kissed the back of his hand. "I know it's way too soon. I know there are lots of logical reasons for me to hesitate about jumping into something so quickly. I know all of these things with my head. My heart is telling me something different."

Owen caught sight of his employees trying to sneak away from the bar without interrupting. He leaned out of the booth and grinned at them. "Merry Christmas, guys. I'll see you on the twenty-seventh."

"Night, boss." Jane ushered the rest of the team to the door before flipping the Closed sign around and locking the door behind her.

"That's subtle." Cole chuckled. "I take it they assume I'm not leaving tonight."

"You've just declared your undying love for me and kissed the back of my hand." Owen stood and pulled Cole to his feet. "You don't understand what you've unleashed."

"Hey now, I don't think I said 'undying love.'"

"No, no, you totally did." Owen didn't stop moving, and Cole stumbled behind him, laughing. "And now I'm taking you to my place for sex. Lots of sex."

Somehow they made it up to his apartment without either of them tripping. It would have been an easier journey if he'd been willing to let go of Cole's hand, but he wasn't. He wasn't taking the chance that Cole would try to get away.

Cole loved him.

And Owen knew deep down in his heart that he loved Cole.

He practically kicked his door open and pulled Cole inside. He didn't know who moved first, but they were kissing within seconds. His body ached from days of hard work and stress, but with Cole's hands on him, it all dissipated.

"You taste like beer," Cole muttered between kisses. "So good."

"You too." He cupped Cole's face with both hands and deepened the kiss. His world spun and narrowed until he was aware of nothing but the man in his arms. Warmth and strength pressed against him, holding him, loving him.

Cole walked him backward until the backs of his legs bumped into the couch. No, he didn't want this time to be here, frantic. He wanted Cole stretched out in his bed, where his scent would linger long after he'd gone.

"Come with me." He grabbed Cole by the front of the shirt and dragged him to bed.

"This is very caveman of you."

"Get used to it."

Clothing was removed between kisses, as he needed to feel Cole's naked skin on his, but was unwilling to relinquish his prize for long. They stumbled and laughed as they stripped each other until they were finally naked.

Perfect.

He couldn't stop touching Cole. He'd thought he'd lost this opportunity, to be with him again. He'd regretted not paying enough attention to this soft spot on Cole's side—he kissed it—or to the back of Cole's knee—he licked it—when they'd been together before. He didn't know what the future held for them exactly, but he wouldn't make assumptions and he wouldn't take Cole for granted again.

He ran his hands up Cole's legs, loving how the muscles twitched beneath his touch. "You're so fucking hot. I never want to let you out of my bed."

"I'm not going anywhere." Cole bucked his hips, making his erect cock sway. "Though I might if you keep teasing me like this."

Owen grinned, his gaze locked on Cole's as he climbed up and finally took Cole's cock into his mouth. The skin was hot and held the bitter flavor of pre-cum. Owen groaned and lapped it up, making sure to tease the crown with his tongue. He knew he'd hit the right spot when Cole bucked his hips and pushed his fingers into Owen's hair.

"God, your mouth." Cole arched off the bed. "So good."

He loved this. Loved the intimacy of a blowjob. Tasting and feeling every twitch of Cole and knowing that he was the one who'd driven him to the edge. Not wanting Cole to come yet, Owen shifted down and began licking long, slow swipes up and down the length of his shaft. When he reached Cole's balls, he teased the puckered skin. It was tempting to lick his ass, bite the insides of his thighs. Tempting, but that wasn't what Owen wanted. No, more than anything he wanted to feel Cole's cock buried deep inside him.

Right now. That's what he wanted.

Cole whimpered when he pulled away. "Where you going?"

"Condom. Lube."

Cole purred and spread his legs wider. "Excellent idea."

When Owen came back from liberating a condom from his bathroom drawer, he tore the packet open and immediately rolled it down Cole's cock as he threw the bottle of lube beside him. He had to laugh at the confusion on Cole's face when Owen climbed over him and turned onto his back. "How do you want me?"

Cole propped himself up on his elbow. "What? I thought . . ."

"I know I haven't given you much indication that I would want to bottom, but I do. I want you"—he reached out and squeezed Cole's cock—"to take this and fuck me. Hard."

Cole closed his eyes and took a slow, deep breath. When Cole opened them again, Owen shuddered at the intensity of his stare. "Get on your hands and knees."

There was no doubting the control in Cole's voice. Owen complied, making sure to spread his legs wide enough to offer support for whatever Cole wanted to do with him. He wasn't surprised at the snap of the lube bottle being opened, nor the cold press of Cole's finger into his ass. What he wasn't expecting was Cole biting down on his ass cheek, or the scrape of Cole's nails into the front of his thigh.

"I can't get enough of you." Cole licked the spot he'd just assaulted. "I get this crazy feeling of wanting to suck and bite and squeeze your skin. I want to press down on you at the same time I ease my way into you. You're making me crazy and obsessive and wild. I'm none of those things."

Owen groaned and let his head fall forward. No one had ever said anything like that to him. Never had he felt that primal connection to another person, man or woman. It was thrilling and terrifying at the same time. Cole was there for him, wanted to reciprocate the care Owen had given him. It was more than sex or friendship. He knew deep down he loved Cole. And Cole loved him the same way.

Thoughts of love and relationships flew from his mind when Cole pushed a second, then third finger into him. Cole stretched him, fucked him with his fingers until he was going insane from want. Words refused to form in his mouth, so instead he began to thrust back against Cole, hoping he'd understand his silent plea.

Cole bit down one final time. "Get on your back. I want to see your face."

He flopped over, a barely controlled fall, and rolled into position. His body shook and a light sheen of sweat now covered his skin. It wasn't going to take long to push him over the edge. From the way Cole's hands shook as he guided his cock between the curves of Owen's ass, he wouldn't be far behind him.

The press of Cole's cock dragged a groan from Owen. It had been so long since he'd done this, been on the receiving end of another man. The intrusion was strange and familiar at once. He had to mentally remind himself to relax, that Cole wouldn't do anything to hurt him, that his body would adjust and the pleasure would come. His cock softened slightly once Cole slid all the way in. Cole wrapped his hand around Owen's cock and gently began to stroke as he peppered him with little thrusts.

It worked. The combination of the two had him hard again within a few minutes. The tension in his body eased as his pleasure grew. Everything dropped away and all he could focus on was Cole: his body, the strength of his thrusts, the gentleness of his caress. When he leaned in and kissed Owen, Owen knew this was everything he could ever want.

Cole broke the kiss, but didn't pull back. "Can you come like this?"

"Yeah. Fuck yeah."

Cole groaned. "Good. I'm going to try and wait for you. I want to feel you squeeze around my cock. I want to feel your cum between us. Like you've done for me."

With each word, Cole thrust harder into him, pushing him closer to the edge. The staccato hits against his prostate took him higher, until he reached the precipice. He opened his eyes and looked up at Cole. He was so close it nearly hurt to see him, so close there was nothing else in his world. So close that he knew he never wanted another person to take Cole's place.

"I love you," Owen whispered a moment before his orgasm slammed into him. He couldn't keep his eyes open then. Waves of pleasure washed through him, tearing him apart from deep inside.

Cole didn't slow down, didn't give him any respite. He thrust harder and faster until Owen couldn't stop from letting out a roar. Another burst of cum spurted between them, coating their bodies. The pleasure threatened to grow painful, but it eventually subsided.

Owen struggled to open his eyes. He saw Cole's face contorted in his own mix of pleasure and pain. His thrusts were erratic and shallow, a move Owen knew all too well. Cole was holding back, trying to draw things out until his orgasm wouldn't be denied. *Poor Cole.* Owen braced his feet against the mattress and squeezed his ass on each thrust. Cole gasped and growled, and his eyes squeezed shut harder.

"Come for me." Owen's voice emerged as barely a whisper. "Come on me."

Gasping, Cole began to pound into him. His prostate was oversensitized now, but Owen refused to move, to do anything that would ruin the moment for Cole. Thankfully, he didn't have to worry long. Within moments, Cole pulled out and ripped the condom off. With a few frantic strokes he threw his head back and cried out. Hot cum landed on Owen's chest and stomach, Cole's cum mixing with his.

Cole sucked in a breath and fell forward onto his hands. With his face hovering inches from Owen's it was easy to see his satisfaction and joy. Owen reached up and cupped his cheek. "I love you."

Cole opened his eyes slowly, blinking several times.

Owen ignored the silence. "There are so many reasons why I shouldn't have said that to you. It's too soon, you're still dealing with Steven, the holidays. But I need you to know. I love you. I want to be a part of your life. This isn't a rebound. This is something more."

Cole leaned down and kissed him softly. "I love you too. I think I have since the first time I walked into the bar and saw you standing there smiling at me."

Owen pulled Cole down and wrapped him in his arms. "Good. Then we're going to take things as they come. I'll listen to you about Steven and work and whatever else you want to talk about."

"And I'm here for you. Not just to talk about what's going on with your dad, but to help you when you need me."

Owen ran his hands through Cole's hair. "Thank you."

After a few moments, he thought Cole had drifted off to sleep. Maybe they both had, because a chill passed through him. Not wanting to move Cole, he grabbed the edge of the blanked and flipped it across them.

"Owen?"

"Didn't mean to wake you. Was getting cold. You good?"

"Couldn't be better. Hey?"

"Hmm?"

"There is something you can do for me."

"What's that?"

"Promise me that if you ever take me bowling, you'll wear your tight pants."

Owen chuckled and held Cole a bit tighter. "Promise."

As he drifted off, he knew that things might not be perfect, but together they'd figure out a way to make it work.

Explore more of our holiday stories for charity!

www.riptidepublishing.com/winter-oranges

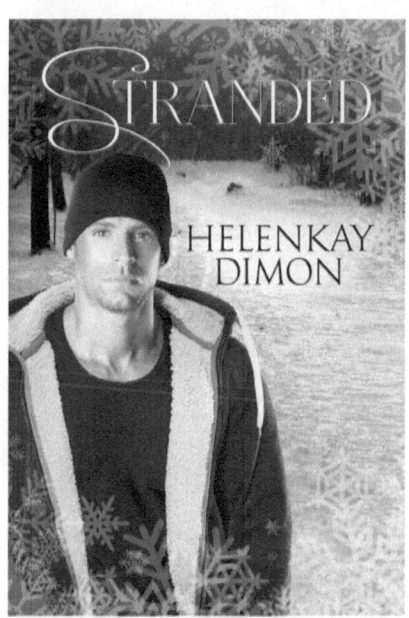

www.riptidepublishing.com/stranded

Dear Reader,

Thank you for reading Christine d'Abo's *Rebound Remedy*!

We know your time is precious and you have many, many entertainment options, so it means a lot that you've chosen to spend your time reading. We really hope you enjoyed it.

We'd be honored if you'd consider posting a review—good or bad—on sites like **Amazon, Barnes & Noble, Kobo, Goodreads, Twitter, Facebook, Tumblr,** and your blog or website. We'd also be honored if you told your friends and family about this book. Word of mouth is a book's lifeblood!

For more information on upcoming releases, author interviews, blog tours, contests, giveaways, and more, please sign up for our weekly, spam-free newsletter and visit us around the web:

Newsletter: tinyurl.com/RiptideSignup
Twitter: twitter.com/RiptideBooks
Facebook: facebook.com/RiptidePublishing
Goodreads: tinyurl.com/RiptideOnGoodreads
Tumblr: riptidepublishing.tumblr.com

Thank you so much for Reading the Rainbow!

RiptidePublishing.com

ALSO BY

*C*HRISTINE D'ABO

ABOUT THE 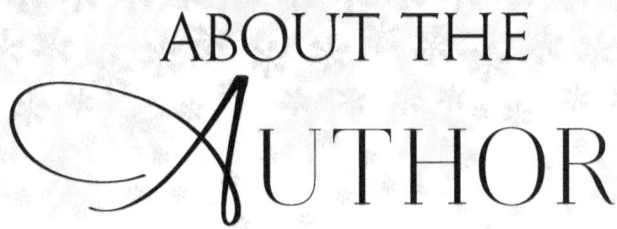AUTHOR

A romance novelist and short story writer, Christine has over thirty publications to her name. She loves to exercise and stops writing just long enough to keep her body in motion too. When she's not pretending to be a ninja in her basement, she's most likely spending time with her family and two dogs.

Website: www.christinedabo.com
Twitter: @Christine_dAbo
Facebook: facebook.com/christine.dabo
Instagram: instagram.com/christine.dabo
Tumblr: christinedabo.tumblr.com

Enjoy more holiday stories at RiptidePublishing.com and give a little help to charity!

Home for the Holidays
ISBN: 978-1-62649-083-3

Christmas Kitsch
ISBN: 978-1-62649-087-1

Earn Bonus Bucks!
Earn 1 Bonus Buck for each dollar you spend. Find out how at
RiptidePublishing.com/news/bonus-bucks.

Win Free Ebooks for a Year!
Pre-order coming soon titles directly through our site and you'll
receive one entry into a drawing for a chance to win free books for
a year! Get the details at RiptidePublishing.com/contests.